Copyright © 2009 Text: Lotte's Rats copyright © 2009 Dan Holloway. Vamos copyright © 2009 Sean Cunningham, Bliss copyright © 2009 Patricia J. DeLois, White Goths copyright © 2009 Roland Denning, The Peter Chair copyright © 2009 Jasper Dorgan, Nothing Changed copyright © 2009 Derek Duggan, Nothing But Grief copyright © 2009 Danny Gillan, Witness copyright © 2009 Gillian E Hamer, Gunfighter Blood copyright © 2009 Larry Harkrider, Tied copyright © 2009 JW Hicks, The Sum of Us copyright © 2009 Amanda Hodgkinson, A G-bag a Day copyright © 2009 JA Hudspith, Beer and Clothing in Hammersmith copyright © 2009 Perry Iles, A Rose for Remembrance copyright © 2009 Lorraine Mace, The Summer They Electrocuted the Rosenbergs copyright © 2009 RK Nathan, Long Legs and Hot Music copyright © 2009 Lawrence Poole, The Reckoning copyright © 2009 Nick Poole, Incompetent Crew copyright © 2009 Jo Reed, Insatiable copyright © 2009 Jane Dixon-Smith, Father Antonio copyright © 2009 James Whyle, Copyright © 2009 Cover illustration: Sean Cunningham

First Edition

The authors assert the moral right under the Copyright, Designs and Patents Act 1988 to be identified as the authors of this work.

All Rights reserved. No part of this publication may be reproduced, stored in a retrieval system, or transmitted, in any form or by any means without the prior written consent of the author, nor be otherwise circulated in any form of binding or cover other than that in which it is published and without a similar condition being imposed on the subsequent purchaser.

Published in 2009 by the copyright holders above.
ISBN 978-0-9561534-0-1

This book is dedicated to the founding members of the Bookshed, and to Edward Smith at the UK Arts Council-funded YouWriteOn.com, for their tireless and enthusiastic shepherding of their respective flocks.

This anthology came about at the fag-end of 2008, following a prolonged period of arguments, fisticuffs and general drunken brawling. The authors, and more just like them, can be found licking their wounds in cyberspace at www.bookshed.eu

CONTENTS

Gunfighter Blood	7
Nothing But Grief	15
The Summer They Electrocuted the Rosenbergs	35
White Goths	47
The Reckoning	63
Beer and Clothing in Hammersmith	71
Lotte's Rats	83
Insatiable	101
The Sum of Us	113
Tied	125
Nothing Changed	137
Father Antonio's Black Label	147
Long Legs and Hot Music	155
A G-bag A Day	167
The Peter Chair	181
Bliss: A Love Story	197
Witness	217
Incompetent Crew	227
Vamos	239
A Rose for Remembrance	249
ABOUT THE AUTHORS	257

Gunfighter Blood

By Larry Harkrider

Describe your family tree. That was our assignment. I wrote about Dublin, Texas—how the blood in my veins came from migrant farmers, originally from Ireland. They endured dust bowls. Great depressions. Grandpa lost a fortune in peanuts, then made it back in turkeys. I exceeded the two page minimum with ease, and used college-ruled paper just to show off. Like any good story, it ended with a bang.

I was nine years old. We were visiting from Boston. It was the last time I saw the old farm—my grandparents both died soon after. We had loaded the car, and were about to leave for the airport. I was hanging out on the front porch, wondering if the rusty tractor could ever be fixed. It'd been parked in the front yard for years. It wasn't really a yard. It was a big clearing on top of a hill, with a dirt road that led to the highway. I remember hearing this awful squawking behind the chicken coop.

I saw the chicken escaping. They had about five chickens. We ate their eggs. It's pretty weird to go into a chicken coop and collect eggs, then eat them. It's even weirder to watch your grandparents grab a turkey by the neck and swing it around until its body flies off. They really do walk around without their heads, you know. It's pretty amazing.

"Janet..."

I glanced up from my paper. The class sat mesmerized. Miss Frey gave me the eye. "It's true," I said. "I swear." She kept giving me the eye. Sixth grade was supposed to be a "nice" place.

Anyhow, this chicken is just walking down the dirt road, heading toward the highway like it's got a plan. I ran after it. Then it started running. Pretty soon I outmaneuvered it, though, and got it going the other direction. We trotted back through our own cloud of dust, back up the hill, back toward the house.

Unfortunately, the chicken got confused and flew into the hog pen. Chickens don't fly very well. It's more like they're flutter-jumping. It got stuck in the mud. The hogs attacked. I got to the fence just as its feathers started flying. I'd always been told to steer clear of the hog pen. Now I knew why. Hogs eat meat. Chicken too. But they didn't just eat that poor chicken. They played tug-of-war.

"Thank you, Janet."

"You'd be surprised by the toughness of chicken," I added, as if it were the story's moral.

"I'm sure that I would. That was very compelling. Now if you could please take a seat."

Nobody clapped. I could tell they were all visualizing that chicken, though. Dublin, Texas would earn high marks. I went to Miss Frey's desk and added it to the growing stack. We were halfway through the alphabet. Dublin Texas, by Janet Kral. Who could top that?

Several boring stories followed. I was more interested in the weird red sunlight filtering through the window. Something was on fire—somewhere. I wanted to see.

I perked up, though, when Patricia Newton got called. She was the only girl taller than me. She got held back a grade, I think. That was the rumor. I found it pretty hard to believe, though. She looked smart. She was also rich. She wore this diamond tennis bracelet. But she didn't show it off, though. She kept her hands in her pockets. Her hair was blonder than mine was black. Her paper appeared to consist of a single sheet. She had not written the minimum two pages. It was on Big Chief Tablet paper too. She had not followed the rules. I could see her primitive block letters showing through, backlit by that smoky red glow. She arched her eyebrows. She gave the paper a little shake to straighten its crease.

"Gunfighter Blood, by Patricia Newton." She cleared her throat with a hard cough. "I come from pioneer types—

not all of them good, including famous outlaws like John Wesley Hardin." She dropped a few outlaw names. Wild this. Crazy that. Hard drinking criminal drunks. "Before all that, we came over from Germany on a boat. That's a good thing, my dad says, cause we would've been a Nazi for sure."

"Patricia?"

"Huh?"

"Do you honestly think that that's appropriate for the classroom?"

Newton looked at the paper, then back at her. "It's the truth. Ask my dad."

"Perhaps I will. Please take a seat."

Newton shrugged and put the paper on Miss Frey's desk. Then she returned to her seat beside the window. She was luckier than me. That red glow had gotten redder. Yeah, there was a fire somewhere.

Things finally got ugly during kickball practice. Newton was showing off. She was the pitcher, and had developed this new move where she would roll the ball toward home plate, then follow along in its wake. This made it hard to kick without hitting her. She was real fast, too, and could catch most kicks with no problem. She kept getting everybody out. Then she would make nasty faces.

Unfortunately for her, I was kickball queen. She was kind of new, and didn't know this important fact. You see, I was usually going half speed. I didn't really want to get sweaty anymore. We were all just going through the motions, pretty much, except for Newton who took it seriously. Someone had to stop her. What happened next was pretty amazing.

If you don't believe my story, then check the yearbook. Kingwood Middle School – 1985.

Don't even bother looking at my "official" photo. Flip to the back. Oh for God's sake.

First of all, nobody told me it was picture day, ok? My mom forgot.

Second, that "photographer" wasn't legit. Seriously, he was a clown. You think I'm joking? He was at your birthday party, idiot. Think about it. Why else would he smell like balloon animals? I'll bet half the balloon animals in Texas had his molester fingerprints. Trust me. He was a clown, and not a nice clown, either. Nah. Clicko is the sort of clown who makes your forehead wrinkle just before—

CLICK—stealing your soul.

Third, I look better in action shots. Forget posing. That's not me. I'm no poser. You wanna see a poser, check Newton's picture. I prefer action, with my hair flying, my teeth gnashing, and egg-shaped kickballs laser-beaming at Newton.

Fuck. It feels like fifteen years ago. I guess it was. Things were so different. We didn't measure ourselves in inches or pounds. How hard could you kick a ball? THAT was the question. Think you can handle my best shot? Think you can catch it? Not a chance. Not back then. Nobody screwed with me. I was a legend.

Seriously. I was invincible. Even when the teachers tried rigging the game, I still found ways to win. No matter how rotten my teammates, I always found a way. That was back when I was really trying of course, when I was new to the school, like Newton, and trying to prove something, like Newton. But unlike Newton, I didn't smash the ball in your face. I played fair. They even tried putting this wheelchair girl on my team, just to even the odds. Oh God, did that ever suck. Don't get me wrong. Alicia Barnes was super cool, and hilarious. She just couldn't play kickball for shit.

Ok, so if you're done laughing at my photo—you ass—flip to page 137. There you will find the photo sequence

I'm talking about.

It's my squad of cripples versus Newton's posers. You will see in frame one that the bases are empty. She was getting everyone out. We were losing six to zero, I think. That's me at the edge of the frame. You will notice that I am removing my heels, and asking to borrow another girl's tennis shoes.

Frame two depicts Newton's high water mark, just before her tragic fall. She has rolled the ball my direction and is following along toward home plate. You can see that I've—changed. I've devolved into a hunched posture. I'm about to permanently re-arrange Newton's menstrual calendar.

Frame three shows Newton sprawled on the ground, clawing at the dirt, searching for her uterus. The ball is not visible. That's because it's in low-earth-orbit, miles above the pitcher's mound. That tiny speck? That's the ball's shadow. That's me rounding second base. I have not broken a sweat.

Frame four shows Newton up on one elbow, trying to figure out why puberty is over. That's me approaching from home plate, hands on my hips, looking down at her.

Frame five is the incredible part. It's the best shot of the bunch. That's me and Newton standing together. We're standing on the pitcher's mound. Talking. We're best friends. Suddenly. That's how it happens. One minute you hate someone. The next? You're wiping gunfighter blood from her lip.

Things changed again when the yearbook came out. She wanted revenge. She got it, eventually. Just think. If some enterprising nerd hadn't taken those photos... It's kind of sad, really.

I later learned that he "loved" me. Right. You might say he was stalking me. He had this sexual fantasy world. I played a starring role. Me and half my friends. Very weird.

I only mention it to explain the photo sequence. Ask me about CATPR sometime, though. I'll tell you all about it.

Nothing But Grief
By Danny Gillan

After a long and arduous search, I finally found myself lying face-down in the gutter.

It would be good if that was a metaphor, because then I wouldn't have been on the verge of drowning in a shallow pool of Glaswegian scum-water.

I spluttered; I squirmed; I . . . (I'm not too proud to admit it) pleaded for my life.

The boot lifted from my back.

'Next time, your face goes through the fucking road,' a voice roared.

'Phlhoo,' I said.

'What?'

I spat the remainder of the puddle-juice from my mouth and said meekly: 'Okay. Sorry, bud.'

'Tell that twat, Kenny, Gerry says it's finished,' my torturer said. 'Understand?'

'Absolutely.' I sat up, arse in the puddle, and ran a hand through my thick but rapidly greying, and slime-slicked, hair.

'Your boss is fucked, and you know what that means for you and the rest of your mates.'

'You're Steph, aren't you?' I asked, putting one hand against a grime-covered wall to steady myself as I struggled to my feet.

'What?'

'You're Steph Madden, from Pardie Street?' I brushed at the front of my shirt with my scratched, wet hands.

'Aye, so?'

'I'm Ped, I knew your brother.'

'Fuck you, you didn't know Jake.'

'I did, actually. He was a good man.' This shirt was for the bin, the trousers too, more than likely. 'What age are you?'

'None of your fucking business.'

'Jake was in my year, so he'd be thirty-three, or he would

have been, if, you know.' I left that hanging, just like my shirt-tails were.

'Don't you fucking talk about Jake.'

'That would make you, what? Thirty-five?'

'So?'

'Just wondering, Steph.'

'Well you can stop fucking wondering. My message to you is this: tell Kenny it's over; he's lost; he's fucked it once too often; Gerry says he's not welcome, anywhere. Understand?'

'Yeah,' I said. 'I understand. I don't really care much, though. Do you?'

'What?'

'My arse is wringin', I'm in a fair bit of pain - thanks for that, by the way - and, as far as I can see, I've got more in common with you than I do with my boss, right at the minute. To be honest, I'd rather just get a pint, if it's all the same to you.'

Steph looked confused. 'Are you acting the cunt?'

'Not as far as I'm aware.'

Steph had hustled me into a lane just off Queen's Drive, outside the park, and the combination of my recent violent dunking and the sharp autumn wind caused me to shiver. I nodded towards the Victoria Arms across the street. 'D'you want a beer?'

'Now I know you're taking the piss.'

'Look, suit yourself. I'm going for a pint and a heat. You've delivered your message and it's been noted, so we've got nothing else to barney about. Frankly, Kenny can take a jump in the Clyde, the way I'm feeling. I just thought you might want a beer in your belly before you head up the road. Your choice, pal.'

'Aye, well, I suppose a pint wouldn't go amiss,' Steph said, hesitantly. 'No nonsense, mind.'

I smiled. 'Not a problem.'

*

Steph had at least four inches on me, up, across and around. We stood, shoulder to upper-arm, at the chipped and pitted wooden bar. It was my district, my invite, which meant it was my round. It was his B.O. I could smell, though, and his dandruff I was trying to get off my shoulder without him noticing.

I ordered two lagers from Tony the landlord. The Vicky is your basic old-man and reprobate's boozer, with few frills and even fewer aspirations. Put it this way - if you encountered a screwdriver in here, which wasn't unheard of, it won't have come from a cocktail list. There were half a dozen punters dotted around the place, every one of them with a half pint of heavy in front of them and a Daily Record opened at the racing pages. Most of the regulars would have left at five to go home for their dinners. The ones that stayed awake would be back by half-six.

'So, Kenny's been a right fuckwit recently, eh?' I said, handing Steph his pint.

'Aye well, Gerry can be a bit of a dopey fucker when he wants,' Steph replied graciously.

'Did you ever wonder what it would be like if we locked the two of them in a room and left them to it?'

Steph let out a short laugh. 'It might be fun.'

I took a deep pull of my lager, draining the glass.

'Same again?' Steph said.

'Aye, cheers.' I stayed quiet while Steph did the honours. 'Cheers, bud,' I said, when he slid my pint over.

'No bother.'

'So, you married, Steph?'

'Oh aye. Wife and three. You?'

'Nah.'

'What, never?'

I paused, debating with myself for a second. 'Nah, never met the right one.'

'Maybe that's no' such a bad thing, eh? Nothing but grief, half the time.'

'Aye. You're right there.' I took a swallow of beer. 'How long have you been working for Gerry, now?'

Steph's drinking arm did an emergency stop before it got to his mouth. 'What's that got to do with anything?'

'Nothing, nothing. Just wondered. This is me fifteen years, with Kenny.'

'Aye well, I'm beating you then. Twenty.'

'Christ.' I paused. 'You ever think we might have been a wee bit young to be joining up for life, back then?'

Steph thought for a moment. 'Ach, I don't know. A job's a job.'

'Aye, but is it a job you want to be doing when you're sixty?'

'Are you fucking joking? I'm no' going to be doing anything till I'm sixty. Have you never heard of a fuckin' pension plan?'

'Fair enough. What about forty, though?'

'Hey, the pension's no' that good,' Steph said. 'More's the fucking pity.'

'It could be,' I said. 'Same again?'

'Aye. What do you mean?'

I waited till I'd got the round in before replying. 'We could do it.'

'Do what?'

'Put them in a room. Kenny and Gerry.'

'What?'

'Think about it. I know I can get Kenny to go anywhere I want. Are you telling me you can't do the same with Gerry? You're his main man, from what I hear.'

A furrow appeared on Steph's brow, not for the first time. 'Aye, maybe. So what?'

'So, I've got plenty of keys to plenty of rooms. So do you. If Kenny's gone, I get all of his keys. You'd be the same, if Gerry was out of the picture.'

Steph looked even more confused, but he was interested. 'Aye but, one of them's still going to be standing.'

'Not necessarily,' I said. 'Have you ever heard of mutually assured destruction?'

Four nights later, Steph and I lay in wait.

Actually, we more sort of lounged in wait.

We were in my Auntie Cassie's living room. Her front window provided ideal viewing for our evening's purpose, and, almost as importantly, she always had nice cakes in.

The room was small but cosy, with the electric fire up at the full three bars. Cassie's cramped second-floor tenement flat had just this room, an even smaller bedroom, a tiny kitchenette and a pokey wee toilet. I'd offered to help Cassie get a nicer place loads of times, but she wouldn't have any of it. She'd lived here since she was twenty-two and wouldn't budge till she couldn't manage the stairs, she said.

'Have a French fancy, son,' my five-foot-nothing aunt said to Steph, proffering a plateful of strikingly coloured, cube-shaped delicacies under his nose.

'Thanks, hen.' Steph took two, a brown and a yellow, and perched them on his bean-bag of a gut. 'Any sign yet?' he asked, from his strategic position on the floral-print sofa, in front of the telly that just happened to be showing the football.

'Not so far,' I said, smiling at my auntie as I lifted a pink cake from the plate and shoved it into my mouth, whole. I was, if I'm honest, also watching the football, albeit from Auntie Cassie's armchair, which at least afforded me a view out of the window.

'Do you boys want a tea or anything?' Cassie asked.

'No, we're fine, Auntie Cass. Thanks, though. We'll let ourselves out if you want to get to your bed.'

'Okay, Peter, son. If you're sure.' Auntie Cassie shuffled out of the room, closing the door behind her. She was one of the good ones, Cassie. She'd pretty much taken over parenting duties when our mum died, and had gone full-time when our old-man drank himself to death a year later. She didn't judge; or ask too many questions.

'That was a shocker, what happened to Jake and his bird,' I said, keeping my eyes on the game.

Steph froze - then, after a second, his shoulders started to tremble.

'I heard they never caught the bastard, is that right?' I said, still watching the 'gers.

'Ped,' Steph said slowly. 'Do us both a favour, and shut the fuck up about my brother, okay?'

'Shit, okay, mate. Sorry.' I glanced out the window. 'Still nothing happening down there.'

This end of the plan was laughably simple, and had proven even simpler to set-up. I told Kenny that Gerry wanted a face-to-face, one-on-one, no weapons, no lieutenants, no worries. One last opportunity to settle things before it got complicated.

Steph had told Gerry a similar tale, only his version included Kenny bringing along a case full of cash and a promise to limit his future activities to the few areas of Glasgow Gerry didn't care about.

I'd chosen a small, self-contained industrial/commercial unit in Rutherglen for the meet, for a number of reasons. One: it was empty and, theoretically, ownerless. Two: it was neutral. Three: it was relatively isolated, there being no other buildings within forty feet of it on any side. Four: It was ugly. Five: it was across the road from my Auntie Cassie's.

Oh, and six: it stood directly above a gas-main.

It takes a lot of work (and bribery) to arrange an accidental gas-main explosion, especially when you have a limited time window.

I was about to find out if I'd managed it.

'They're here,' I said.

Steph lumbered over from the sofa and joined me at the window. We watched together as two black-hacks approached from opposite directions and pulled up in front of the single-story concrete building. I was impressed with their timing, it has to be said.

Gerry's tall, slim figure got out of one cab, and Kenny, smaller vertically but twice as wide horizontally, exited the other. Steph and I watched as they nodded an awkward acknowledgement to each other and walked stiffly towards the door.

They had a maximum of twelve feet to cover, but they still managed to turn it into a pantomime; the exact opposite of a race. Neither of them wanted to get ahead of the other, but, equally important, they couldn't allow themselves to fall behind. They ended up starting and stumbling, stopping and starting, they looked like Laurel and Hardy, until they got to the door.

My eyes were on Kenny, obviously. I was supposed to be on his team. Gerry, I didn't give a toss about.

They made it inside and Steph and I saw the light come on through the wire-mesh covered window.

'How long?' Steph asked.

'How long what?'

'How long do we wait?' Unfortunately, we couldn't remain objective observers in this particular passion play. We had a task or two to complete ourselves.

'Oh, right. Sorry,' I said. 'Do you want to, or should I? Anytime now would be good.'

'Fuck's sake, Ped. Don't crap out now.' Steph looked more scared than worried.

'Sorry, I know. I'm on my way.' I looked Steph in the eye. 'This is it, are you sure you're up for it? Last chance.'

'Fuck him. He's never been that good to me. He thinks he has, but he's a cunt.' Steph paused and gave me a serious look. 'Blow the fucker to fuck.' I think, ultimately, it was his eloquence that I found so endearing.

'On it.' I headed for the front door and trotted briskly down the stairs to the street.

At nine-thirty on a Saturday night King Street was deserted. There were no chip-shops or off-sales on this road, so all the local neds were either up on Main Street looking for a pub or in Toryglen, scouting for a fight. Everyone else was watching the X-Factor.

I crossed the street and took up position outside the door of the squat, bunker-like building. I could hear the low murmur of voices from inside as I fished in my jacket pocket and found the mortice-key. I inserted it gingerly through the keyhole and, quiet as a priest with a porn habit, turned it to the left.

This particular mechanism was well-oiled; I'd made sure of that. The click as the door locked was barely audible. I removed the key and held my breath for a few seconds, fight-or-flight gland fully engaged. The timbre of the voices inside didn't change.

I looked up towards Auntie Cassie's window. I could just make out Steph's hulking form behind the net-curtains, and gave a thumbs-up. Stage one successfully completed. Time for stage two.

The thing about a gas-main explosion, however pre-arranged it may be, is that it still needs a spark to set it off.

I've got a Zippo.

I checked my watch - nine-forty-four. Billy at the power plant had agreed to allow the pressure to build up in this particular main for exactly sixty seconds, any longer and it would be traceable. We agreed on nine-forty-five to nine-forty-six.

I shuffled my arse carefully along the ground, below

the small window. I reached the grey box embedded in the grass that housed the gas meter. I retrieved the small wing-key Billy had given me from my other jacket pocket, and opened the lid.

On the meter, five white and two red numerical reels measured the amount of gas passing through this particular system. I noted with satisfaction that the two red reels were spinning pretty bloody quickly.

Behind the meter, I could see a two-inch pipe leading into the building in question. This gap was the key to the whole thing. The seal should have been made with heat-resistant zirconium. Equally, there wasn't supposed to be any space between the pipe and the concrete below.

It seemed Steph and I had spent our money well, though. At least three-inches of space existed between the bottom of the pipe and the (recently drilled) concrete.

I poked a finger at the pipe's seal, where it exited the gas meter. It gave. I don't have the first clue what the hell zirconium is, but I'm fairly sure it's not supposed to feel like putty.

I brought out my brass Zippo and flicked it open.

For the first time, it occurred to me that I was going to have to sacrifice my lighter. I wished I'd thought of this earlier and bought another to use. My sister gave me this one as a thirtieth birthday present. It meant something. Still, the greater good.

I thumbed the blackened wheel for the last time, and held the beast in front of me as the flame caught. It's a damned fine piece of machinery, the Zippo.

I'm not ashamed to admit that I said a brief prayer before placing my flaming torch beneath that two-inch pipe.

Then I ran away. Like fuck.

Billy reckoned it would take around thirty-seconds for the flame to cut through the compromised seal. To me, it felt like hours.

It's not every day you kill someone. This is not a bad thing. Even when your job might potentially involve it, it shouldn't be every day, or everyday, for that matter. Some are worse than others, though.

I made it back up to Cassie's living room before it blew and got to watch. It was quite Moroccan, lots of burnt orange, etc.

'Hah!' Steph shouted. 'Dead, dead, fucking dead! Who's got the keys now? Who's got the fucking keys now, eh? Eh?'

He tried to hug me, but I didn't let him.

There were days (and this was very much one of them) when I hated being an Estate Agent.

My aunt scurried into the living room in her ankle-length nightie and pink bed-socks when she heard the blast, and was hunched at the window, wide-eyed as she surveyed the damage across the road. 'We weren't here, Cassie. Okay?'

'Aye, son, nae bother.' She was too engrossed by the sight of tomorrow's gossip to look round as Steph and I left.

We went back to the Victoria Arms - much busier than it had been on our last visit - and this time it was Steph's turn to get the first round in. I ordered a port. Lager wouldn't cut it tonight.

Steph had almost managed to bring his excitement under control as I caught Tony's eye and leaned over the bar.

'We've been in here since seven, Tony,' I said quietly.

'No worries, Ped.' Tony winked and returned to his duties without another word.

'Jesus, Ped,' Steph said, draining half his pint in one go. 'Tomorrow, we control it all. All the shops, all the sites, all the contracts. They're all ours! Fucking hell, cheers mate.' He downed the rest of his beer.

I ordered another round. Port and a whisky chaser, this

time.

'There you go, bud.' I passed Steph his pint.

'Cheers,' my new business partner said, a huge grin on his face.

I shook my head. Killing two people wasn't this easy. It's the hardest thing in the world. You shouldn't be happy afterwards. There should at least be some regret, it was only natural. Steph's un-tempered delight disappointed me, frankly.

'Does it bother you at all that you've just murdered the guy who's been paying your wages for twenty years?'

Steph's smile faltered. 'How d'you mean?'

'They're dead, Steph. Gerry and Kenny are crispy bacon. Don't you have a wee touch of remorse? Don't you think we should at least be feeling a bit reflective?'

He looked even more confused. 'This was your fucking idea, Ped. You set it all up, you lit the fucking fuse.'

That was true, I supposed. Didn't mean this moron deserved to be joyous. 'Sorry, bud. I've just got the post explosion jitters.'

'Aye, well. Get it under control. D'you want to give the fucking game away?'

I'd had enough. 'What was Jake's girlfriend's name, again?' I said, downing my whisky.

'What?'

'Jake's bird, the one that got, you know, killed with him. I can't remember her name,' I lied.

'Allison. Why?'

'Allison, that's right. Wee lassie, red hair. What was her second name? It's on the tip of my tongue.' I looked at Steph blankly as his brain attempted to work.

'Doyle, it was Allison Doyle, I think,' Steph's eyebrows formed a v-shape. 'Why?'

I held his gaze for a second, wondering if he had been paying attention. Had he noticed the nameplate on Auntie

Cassie's front door?

Cassie was my dad's sister. Unlike me, she had never married.

But no, nothing. Steph was as clueless as a drunk arsonist should be.

'Sorry, mate,' I said. 'Don't know why that came up. They'd been running around together for a while though, hadn't they?'

'Aye, a few months. She was a bit secretive, but a nice kid.'

'Secretive? Maybe she was married or something, eh?' I smiled.

'Eh, no, I don't think so,' Steph said. 'We all thought they were going to do well.'

'I bet you did. It's a real shame that didn't work out.'

'Yeah, a shame.' Steph's shoulders sank and his head bowed.

That's regret, you prick, I thought.

'It was a knifing, wasn't it?'

Steph looked up sharply. 'So?'

I could feel the shape of the knife pressing against my chest from the inside-pocket of my jacket as I leaned towards Steph. The knife was a present from my sister too, part of a set. A wedding present.

'Just wondering, Steph,' I said, giving myself a shake. 'That got a bit heavy, sorry bud.'

'A bit?' Steph sighed with relief. 'Fucking hell, Ped, you had me worried for a minute.'

'Yeah, sorry about that.'

'Fucking chill out, mate. We own the world, be fucking happy. I need a jimmy riddle, get the beers in.'

I watched Steph go to the gents. I ordered another round (double port, double whisky). I stood there. I drank the port, ignored the whisky. I thought about it.

Betrayal of trust, lack of loyalty. It was . . . unattractive.

It deserved redress. And killing two people wasn't fucking easy.

I went to the gents.

Steph stood, pissing into a urinal. He turned to say hello, an almost ecstatic look on his face.

I took the knife out of my pocket and shoved it into his right kidney.

His body spasmed and jerked backwards, piss still flowing. It formed a yellow, rearward arc, and hit me in the eye. That was okay.

Killing people shouldn't be easy, it shouldn't be pleasant.

It's dirty work. An eye full of piss was fair enough, I reckoned, as I lowered Steph's carcass to the manky, urine-soaked floor.

Jake hadn't been simple or quick. Allison had fought like a banshee.

I took my knife back (it was a gift, after all), and removed the mortice-key from my jacket. I grabbed some paper towels from the dispenser and wiped the piss from my eye, then the blood from my knife, then my prints from the key. I bent down and put the key into Steph's trouser pocket.

I left the toilet and forced my way through the crowd, gesturing to Tony when I reached the bar.

'Change of plan, Tony. I haven't been in here at all tonight, okay?'

Tony gave me a quizzical look. 'Aye, okay Ped. No bother.'

'Thanks mate. Do me a favour and wash those glasses next, eh?' I pointed at the port and whisky tumblers I'd left on the bar.

'What about your pal?' I heard Tony call as I pushed through the punters and hurried out to the street.

I wanted to puke, but had seen enough CSI to know they might be able to get DNA from it, so I held it in till

I was a good quarter-of-a-mile away from the pub. Then I let fly in a bin-lane.

Killing people shouldn't be easy, and it wasn't. Now and then, though, it had to be done.

I wandered up Pollokshaws Road and on to Shawlands. The bars and curry-houses were packed, and I had just about enough spatial-awareness left to avoid the various steamers and smokers crowding the pavements.

I felt dizzy. Was this really my new job description - knife-killer, mad-slasher, bomber?

I wanted to be a vet when I was a kid.

After an hour or so, I felt calm enough to speak. I dialled a number on my mobile and arranged a lift home, then sat on a bench outside Queen's Park.

Ten minutes later, a black BMW pulled up. The front seats were occupied, and I pulled myself up wearily and got into the back.

'Is it done?'

'Yeah, it's done,' I said. 'All of it.'

'How was it?'

'How do you think? It was fucking horrible. But it's done.'

As we drove, I remembered my wedding day. It was only ten months previously. Nothing had faded, but everything had changed.

Allison looked beautiful, as always, and had a smile so wide it could have cracked a diamond.

Given the circumstances it was, by necessity, a small, non-church affair, only twenty-five guests in all. Auntie Cassie was crying into her satin hankie before it even started.

Allison looked like a goddess walking down the short aisle of the registry office. She held the confidence of her youth, the strength of her beauty, and the certainty of her intelligence in every step.

As we stood facing the waiting registrar, she broke from tradition and leaned towards me. 'Good luck, you,' she whispered.

'Cheers doll,' I said, winking at her as she sidled away and took her seat in the front row, next to Auntie Cassie.

Jake stepped forward and clasped my hand nervously.

Jake and I were, I think, the fifty-fourth couple to be joined in a civil partnership in Scotland since the law changed.

We had tossed a coin to see who would be 'given-away'. I'd won, and had then had to toss another one to decide between Cassie and Allison. I was secretly glad that my wee sister won, but I'd never tell Cassie that.

Allison had volunteered to play the part of Jake's girlfriend in public. His family, and especially his brother, would never have been able to cope with his being gay. Allison thought it was funny.

It wasn't funny, anymore.

'It had to be done.'

'I know. Doesn't mean it was easy,' I said. We were driving through Rutherglen. 'You're not actually going to have a look, are you?'

'Hey, you've got to look,' Kenny said from the driver's seat.

I shook my head. Some people were just morbid.

The police had coned-off the lane nearest the blast-site to provide space for the three fire-engines, and a harassed yet bored looking PC was directing traffic.

We had a decent view of the remains as we waited for permission to pass. The concrete-block of a building was gone, bar a foot or so of blackened steel-mesh jutting and twisting out of the ground to mark the foundations.

Despite my mood, I gave myself a mental pat on the back. In contrast to the utter devastation inflicted on the target structure, there didn't appear to be any damage to the surrounding tenements, not even superficially. I owed Billy a couple of pints.

'Good job, son,' Kenny said.

'Aye, cheers boss. Glad you got out in time. Can we go now?'

''Course we can.' The plod waved us on and we sped off towards Cambuslang.

Jake managed to make one call on his mobile before he bled to death on that cold pavement in Govan, after he'd watched helplessly as Allison took her last earthly breath six-feet away from him.

I'd been busy at a viewing and didn't pick up. This fact destroys me a little bit more every day.

'It was Steph, he found out,' he'd gasped. 'He doesn't know about you . . . but he knows I'm gay . . . and about Allison lying. He went crazy. Oh Jesus, Allison . . .' that was all he said before the line went dead. It was three hours later that I listened to my messages.

That one, I saved.

The car pulled up outside my house.

'This is you, son,' Kenny said.

I looked through the car window at our, sorry, my home. It was a semi-detached, two-storey, three-bedroom, two-garden, one-garage, no-personality, box. We'd liked it. I hated it. It had become the loneliest hole on the planet.

'Do you guys want to come in for a drink?' I really didn't feel like being alone.

'If you're asking. What do you reckon?' Kenny looked towards the passenger seat.

'Aye, the boy deserves some company,' Gerry said.

They weren't enemies. That's what Steph never understood. They were competitors - that's different.

They were both estate agents, they were both property developers, and yes, they sometimes got in each other's way and had a problem. But it was a business problem. They were business men.

We had all, Kenny, Gerry, Steph and me, started life on the wrong side of the law, that was certainly true. But the ridiculous profit-margins to be made on property quickly made any (or most) illegal activities redundant.

I passed out the whisky.

A deal had been made, an accommodation arrived at.

Kenny owned the deeds to an ugly but listed, and therefore protected, building in Rutherglen. Kenny owed Gerry a few grand. I gave them both a key to the back door.

I blew-up the listed building, and Kenny gave Gerry the site for development. Gerry got to build the flats, and everyone was happy.

And I got to deal with Steph.

From the day he found out what Steph had done to Jake and Allison, Gerry wanted rid of him. He was decent enough to offer, through Kenny, the opportunity to me.

I had to be sure, though, before I could go through with it. I had to get close enough to Steph to convince myself that he was, indeed, an animal capable of killing those closest to him.

Plus, we needed someone to pin the 'accident' on if the law got suspicious.

Neither Kenny nor Gerry had been particularly enamoured with their allotted roles in my plan, especially when they found out how tight the timing would be, but they had agreed to do it, out of respect and friendship. They were decent men, and they didn't judge.

'What are you feeling, kid?' Kenny said gently, sitting

next to me on the sofa and draping an arm around my shoulder.

I tried to smile. 'Nothing but grief, boss. Nothing but grief.'

The Summer They Electrocuted the Rosenbergs

By R.K. Nathan

Mom always has to be right. Even when someone forces her to admit that she's wrong, she still unearths a way to shine some happy light upon herself. As far as I can see, Dad just gave up answering back six or seven years back, before the 70s even began. Now he spends practically all his time at work. Sometimes he surprises us by coming home to eat dinner with us, cracking jokes from the same list that never changes, and sometimes he even takes us to the movies, when there's some stupid disaster film he wants to see. But when Mom is busy being right, he just stays away from us. Which means she can be right about him ignoring us because he's a coward, because he's a doom-monger, because he's a (whisper this one) fake... She can be right when she rails about our table being spurned by its patriarch. And this summer she gets to be right much more often, because for some reason summer camp has been taken off the menu and so I have to spend most of my time listening to her. I try to find reasons to stay longer in my room; she tries to break them all down.

"We have to go now, young lady!"

"Coming!" Closing my diary quickly, I push it back under the bed, lifting it above the line of the shag pile so it'll go a little further and not be visible to any but the very snoopiest. Mom would do plenty, but she wouldn't lie on the floor. Heaven help me if she ever found it and saw that I was no genius after all.

"But not quickly enough. Come quickly!" Then she has another thought and knows immediately she has to add it. "But never hurry."

"I won't hurry, Mom."

She loves to use up my holidays by taking me around to her friends' houses. I tell her to leave me behind, but she refuses. I hate it when she draws attention to my still-tiny breasts and my not-so tiny zits like they were some kind of achievement. The slow blinks her friends send back at me seem kind of sympathetic. Poor girl; takes after her daddy in the face and legs. Mom loves to say that in as many words, always more or less presenting her own face and legs to them for comparison. God help Mom, I think, if her only daughter hadn't been such a slow developer.

Then I realise the only daughter is me, and the slow developing thing is kind of a cross. Laughing about it is supposed to be healthy, but it's also pretty screwed-up at the same time.

Her friends are mostly pretty too, in that magazine-left-in-the-shop-window kind of way, and they all wear their summer dresses without ever bothering to sideglance at all the mirrors they pass. Their breasts don't have to be fleetingly glimpsed; they can just be. Meanwhile Mom defines the whole world around us by where its mirrors happen to be placed.

As we line up in the little jam that always fills the on-ramp to the freeway, she turns the rearview toward herself and blows away a stray eyelash. A few seconds go by as she keeps staring. The mirror tells her things, I guess, like the one in Snow White. The traffic starts to move again.

"Where exactly are we going, Mom?"

"Today we're going to see Marguerite." The man in the Camaro beside us is honking his horn because Mum is halfway between lanes. She smiles grandly at him and stays right where she is. He keeps honking. "Remember she has a son your age?"

"Yeah, I remember." My voice is leaden. What was his name – Johnny or Donny? Only his hands moved quicker than his mouth. He forgot my name three times and told me I was frigid and a prick teaser. How could I be both, I asked him. He shook his head at me the same way Mom often did. They learned that from the same place, I'm sure: the school of getting your own way. A year on I could just tell that he would probably be much the same but with more zits. His room would still stink of hormones and laziness. Boys who start out predictable get even more so.

Mom's friends always receive us, never vice versa. This is because their houses are that little bit bigger than ours; most of them live in Westchester County or Connecticut. They have gardens, terraces, dining rooms and an upstairs floor. Some even have gables. Mom's friends smirk at the idea and mention of Brooklyn, but usually quickly and, I noticed, only when Mom's in the bathroom.

When we go to over to their places for drinks or afternoon tea, I never ask these women questions, because they don't seem to like questions that much. They usually like to keep their dreams to themselves, but of course Mom won't let them get away with that. She makes them dust them off and share them. Actresses have to relive, maybe even recite, their great lines. Dancers have to move gracefully across a room for her. Writers have to talk about the torrents of ideas that still come to them when they least expect it. And they actually do these things for her – she's pretty persuasive that way, my Mom.

"Hi Marguerite!" Mom cries. "You're looking hysterically good, girl! Not since we were at Smith. What in God's name have you not been eating!" Now she points at me and I fight back the automatic shudder this triggers. "See, your arms are getting like Sylvia's!"

Marguerite turns to give me the same vacant blue blink as ever. "So good to see you, Sylvia." Now she remembers something and warms up. "Oh, there's a surprise here for you, you know."

A surprise. I look down so I don't have to respond to the sleazy little look that's entering her eye. Their shag pile carpet, thicker than ours, hides my toes. I can almost picture her beside me, grabbing my hip and trying to push Donny's leathery tongue past my tightly-shut lips. She could kiss the little slob herself, couldn't she, if it was really all that necessary?

"Hello, Mrs Bernstein. It's, uh, cool to get surprises. Mostly."

"You'll see!" she cries, widening her eyes for me. It's not sympathy now. It's just relief that she's done the job she told herself she had to do.

"Sylvia's staying home and writing this summer. Instead of going to the camp with the others."

"That's great, Sylvia! You can show some of what you've been writing to your surprise. He just loves to read. Oh no, I've gone and given away that it's a boy!"

Whenever Dad says Marguerite used to be a chorus girl, Mom sniggers and tells him not to be mean. All Mom's friends are artists, you see. They all have to be considered first before they can be dismissed.

"See," begins Mom, "Sylvia got this great opportunity to use what we know and to not make the same mistakes as we…"

"Mistakes?" Marguerite almost frowns. "I think luck has a great part…"

Mom's eyes and nostrils are already flaring against being contradicted. It looks like hard work for her eyelids to push up all that liner. "Oh of course it does, but all the changes in our times have made it so much more, uh, possible."

Marguerite nods silently instead of risking saying something else that might suggest that Mom is wrong. I used to love it when Mom conducted her friends like an orchestra, but now I want her to listen to herself a bit more. Marguerite goes to the table and gets us some drinks – vodka and tonic for Mom and a ginger ale for me.

"Who else is coming, Marguerite?"

"Lucy's coming by. She also has a boy now, a stepson."

"The new man had a boy already?"

"A boy? He's seventeen, you know. She jumped straight to being mother of a teenager, practically a man already. I saw them parking up just a moment ago."

Mom starts to clap her hands but stops before they made a sound. "Oh my, they'll be fighting over the damsel."

"Please, Mom!"

I move closer to the window. Through the double glazing I can see a sliver of the lake, while from above me an icy finger curls out of the air conditioning ducts and taps my forehead, telling me that I really am crazy. The cold is pleasant; it makes me feel far away from all this fakery. I see that the ducks are lazily following one another around, today seemingly bored by their easy lives. Usually they seem pretty content. A young boy without a shirt chases another and they are both yelling something stupid that echoes around the little park.

"You should've seen what she's been writing. We went down to Big Sur at Easter and I gave her The Bell Jar as a present because I thought it was about time I should. And I told her as well."

"You told her about us at Smith?"

"That's right: about the class we took. About what it all meant."

Driving around Big Sur, while Dad tried to find some pointless ball game on the radio, Mom told me all about my name and described what she called my genesis. I had no idea I had a genesis. Most people are just born; I had to be created. She explained in lots of words that I was created about the same time the Bell Jar book was being created. What was I supposed to say to that?

I thanked her. She got angry.

She made me read that book right away, sitting out on the terrace of the house we were staying in and when we came back to Brooklyn she made me start writing for myself. First I wrote something garbled about the "diamond smarts of the streets of New York" but really they didn't mean anything to me. Those streets were so full of people stealing space from one another that it felt like all the meaning had been squeezed out of them. I read the book by my namesake again and again about that poor girl who was struggling with all her myriad possibilities at once. Mom was so unlike that girl it was unreal. How could I take all her arguments seriously? Mom wrote poetry about her feelings and I'd never seen any of those feelings actually come out in real life; only faking a fake life there on the page.

"Sylvia Plath was your teacher that year, wasn't she?"

"Four of us from that class are still friends – me, Marguerite, Lucy and Jane. And the children we had. Or acquired."

Now Marguerite has a curious look circling inside her eye and I can feel hot breath on my neck. I swivel slowly. Donny (I remember now, last year I kept calling him Boy Osmond) has braces now and is getting blockier. Death for a sixteen year old. It's clear he's going to be a chubby adult and more often than not his clammy hands will be stopped from roaming. Stopped dead, told to go home and touch himself instead. And he'll have to go.

"Hi, Sylvia. We been expecting ya." Behind him is a taller and quieter boy who right away seems a bit more intriguing. "Uh, this is Ricky."

"Nice to meet you," says Ricky. "I've heard, uh, you know, stuff. Good stuff." His handshake is shy but still pretty firm. His eyes, dove-blue instead of vacant-blue, are looking at my face instead of my breasts.

"Is this the surprise?" I ask quietly.

Marguerite understands these moments better than Mom. Her mouth is already making an extremely disappointed shape. "Whatever you prefer it to be," she says, trying to sound vague.

Right then, something in Marguerite's resigned tone makes me feel a little bolder. Sometimes I really do get to choose what I want, it seems. Sometimes I really do get to make the others react to me. I don't always have to follow the leader. Or follow Mom. "And so I was the only one of your kids who got to be called Sylvia?"

Sensing the criticism in my voice, Mom sniffs at me, "I was the only one brave enough to consider us an epoch. To mark it with a child of mine."

"Wouldn't it have been better to write a book?" I ask her. I can feel that I am overstepping the bounds she has always laid down for me so painstakingly, while still demanding that I break other people's rules. I can feel that I'm angering her, and I absolutely love the thrill this is giving me.

"Who says I didn't? Books get published or they don't. They still have to be written. You should just concentrate on writing your own."

But I knew I wasn't going to write a book. Not this year and certainly not a book like The Bell Jar. Summers weren't sultry and queer to me; they were long and desperate, full of wrong turns and dead hours and lying dreams. But the Rosenbergs still got electrocuted every time I read that book, as did Sylvia's alter ego. It was jerky, unkempt. I had the idea that Mom would have been happier if it was me down on the chair, succumbing to some kind of treatment that at least showed I was special to begin with. Mom would never have wanted to be electrocuted herself, but if it could be her daughter who was artistic and wayward and doomed, then that might be some kind of a divine and liveable result.

"What was she like as a teacher?" I ask. I can smell that the boys have been sneaking some vodka into their ginger ale, or maybe that was Marguerite. All the breath around me is sour and flammable.

"Pretty lousy actually," says Marguerite without stopping to think.

Now Mom bursts to life again, defending her own

version of the universe.

"Her writing was absolutely extraordinary!" she exclaims. And she is right the way she is always right. Marguerite and Lucy nod a little at what she is saying, perhaps at what she is upholding too. But I can't help wondering if that extraordinary writing that by chance she got so close to learning from has told her to go and outrun her ordinariness by just passing the hot potato on to me. It's my responsibility now, not hers. Mom sighs, looking for an amazing thing to say. Everyone is listening to her. "Her life was tragic. Well, it was!"

Most of the ducks are back out on the water, bobbing towards the bridge, where the two kids have stopped running and are ready to start throwing stones. I have never wanted a brother, but sometimes start to thinking that maybe a brother would have served a purpose.

"Can you get me some more ginger ale?" I ask Ricky, turning my shoulder towards Donny and squeezing him out of our little corner. Ricky still comes across as a touch shy and studious, like me, it's true, but a girl can get away with that kind of thing if she knows when to sugar her voice and when to stay quiet.

"Sure." He takes my glass and goes to fill it, more eager to please than anyone I have seen since school finished three weeks ago. That look of acquiescence is like what Dad used to give me years ago, when he was the big bear letting his little Goldilocks have something her own way. It's something I have to win back, but the evidence at least suggests it isn't gone from the world entirely.

"Let's go listen to some music, guys," says Donny. He has home-field advantage; the record player is in the corner of his grotty room upstairs, with Kiss and Farrah Fawcett all over the walls and scads of wadded tissues under the bed.

"You go, we'll catch you up later," I nod, turning to

Ricky, who's coming back with my drink. "First I'd like to go out to the lake for a while. Let's leave our moms to talk about the other Sylvia again. Or whatever they want."

"Okay," says Ricky, handing me the glass.

"But..." begins Donny, outflanked and betrayed. He can see the shape of failure already, when usually his great advantage in life is that failure is something he refuses to picture, however inevitable it may really be. He's starting to lose for real.

"Later, Donny, later. Pick out some cool LPs for us. Not that Rick Wakeman thing you played last year! It was dreck! Bye Mom, bye Marguerite, bye Lucy!"

I carry the glass of ginger ale in one hand as I haul open the sliding glass door with the other. The ice cubes clink against the rim of the glass. Hot air rushes in and Ricky follows me close behind, holding some ginger ale of his own, charged up with extra vodka. I close the door behind us and look back in to see Mom staring at me through the glass. It's not surprise I can see in her eyes, not really, but suddenly it seems like there's an angle she forgot to consider somewhere. She is trying to retrace the landscape she knew so well this morning and some details are missing from it.

Mom still knows she's right, of course, but I think she realises now that getting me to think so too might just be getting that little bit harder all the time. While she realises that, I realise that Dad is already lost to her. And if she stops being able to convince the two of us just like that, she might just have to work at convincing the others as well.

Life might just crumble around us. And the right kind of boys might just start to like me, after all. Who knows?

Ricky touches my elbow and, sparking against one another, we walk over towards the bridge, as dreamily as the ducks did. The two younger boys see us coming and run off to find a patch of the little park that's all for them and whatever they want from life.

The ducks, on the other hand, leave the bridge and make straight for us, gliding across the peaceful lake, cutting deeply into its mirror image of the sky with the cleanest V-shaped wake I have ever seen.

White Goths

By Roland Denning

Nothing was the same after we drank Jonni's blood.

It's gone now, but you may have walked past our shop if you wandered through the labyrinths of Camden Lock market a year or two ago. If you ever saw yourself as a bit of a Goth you'd have been inside. It was more a cross between a stall and a cave than a shop, a gloomy little hole set deep into the tunnels where they used to lead the horses, the horses that pulled the barges along the canal. Jonni said the ghosts of the horses whinnied in the night but I never heard them.

Everyone loved Jonni. It was what every Goth shop needed, a sweet wraith of a boy with almost translucent skin and big eyes set deep into the shadows; a delicate kid with just a few rough edges and a wobbly smile that made you want to either hug him or cry. He was the perfect Goth and he never even wore make-up. I asked Jonni once what it meant to be a Goth. He lay back on his bed and thought for a moment then said:

'It's just a little space we make where we can dream. That's all. But that's enough to make people hate us.'

Jonni was a junkie, of course. Everyone knew, no one made a thing of it. And yeah, I fancied him. All the girls did. But nothing physical happened with us. Physically, Jonni never seemed quite there.

It was just the three of us who ran the shop: me, Jonni and Matty. Matty was the oldest and the one with the cash, the one who started the business. Some people said he was just a burnt out old hippie in a pirate outfit; all right, he was an old hippie in a pirate outfit, but there was something calming about him. He spoke slowly, which some took as being wise, but I took as just wanting to be wise. And that's something; better than wanting to be stupid, which is how many kids today play it. But Matty was an anchor, and you need one of those in these dark seas. I sort of liked Matty, but I never took him as seriously as he took himself.

I asked Matty what he thought it meant to be a Goth too, and he was pleased that I asked because he had spent a lot of time writing down the answers in his notebook.
  'It's like the whole of life is all about getting dressed up for a big event, we all think we're getting ready for this grand ball. Goths do too; it's just that we know who's going to be there.'
  And then he gave this knowing smile, like he had said something really clever.

Most of the shop was filled with racks of clothes but in the back were little cubby holes, shelves cut into the old brickwork and cupboards with no doors that we let get really dusty. We added some fake cobwebs too and tiny red light bulbs in the corners. They were our display cabinets, but most of the stuff in there was just for effect, window dressing, really. Murky jars and bottles and all sorts of weird specimens, like bones and crucifixes and, amongst them, the chalices and candlesticks and rings with skulls on that we actually sold. Half the things had been there so long that even we didn't know what they were. It was in one of those places we kept Jonni's blood.

Sometimes journalists and TV people, after a teenage suicide or a high school shooting at some hick town in the States, would come into our shop and ask us what Goths actually did, what it was all about. And I'd just give a mysterious smile, a smile that says we're part of something, and you're not while they stared deep into my lace-up purple basque. And there wasn't anything much to say, really, about what we did; just being a Goth is a full time job, getting the make-up right could take all day (unless you were Jonni), you don't have time for much else. Just making it seem we shared a big secret was good in itself, and when you've found people who think and feel the same way you do, there's no need for explanations.

The blood thing was never serious with Jonni. It started one day when he gashed his hand on a sharp point of a coat hanger. He laughed as he let his blood drip into this tiny glass phial then put a cork in the top. I think the phial had been a perfume sample or something, but Jonni clasped it like it was something special, our first reliquary.

'We're going to keep this,' he said. 'It might be worth something one day.'

And that was it, just a little joke of Jonni's, and he put the phial of blood at the back of the shelves so a red light glowed through it. Of course, there wasn't much blood to begin with, but Jonni topped it up over the next few weeks, with a pin prick to the finger or a razor to his arm. I suppose some people call that self-harming, but to us it was just one of Jonni's little games. He never felt any pain, not with all the smack running through his veins, so I don't know if you'd really call it 'harm'.

But drinking Jonni's blood... it was Lester, of all people, who actually did it first. We'd all talked about it, specially in front of Lester, trying to freak him out. Or test him. Like we all thought Lester was just too straight; I suppose we wanted to prove that we were real Goths and he was just a Yankee fake. We never thought he'd take the idea seriously.

We all knew Lester was desperate to work in the shop, but no one thought he was right, even though we often needed him. Lester could find things, he could get stuff. If we ever ran low on stock, like skull rings, Lester knew a cheap supply. We think he scored Jonni's drugs for him too, but we were never sure. We were always too cool to ask Jonni about his drugs.

Matty said there were three things wrong with Lester and I agreed: first he smiled too much, second he was a punk, third he was American. The first and third were probably connected, like he was into being positive, and that doesn't really go with the Goth vibe. But I have to say he looked great as a punk, even though he was a control freak, and real punks just want to get out of control.

Yeah, Lester looked great as a punk with his scarlet Mohican and, although it pains me to admit it, when the time came, even better as a Goth. He didn't turn Goth till Jonni had gone, when he started working in the shop full time. He never had Jonni's style, Jonni's authenticity; with Lester you always had a sense he was acting rather than living it, playing a part. But, fuck, did he play it well. Sure, he always looked way too healthy, he couldn't get rid of that smile but he learnt the trick of shifting it so it looked sort of quietly demonic. He was thin and tall and had this black suit, with a long jacket tight around the waist but flaring out at the top and bottom that made him look like a gangly cartoon vampire. He never lost that punk way of bouncing around, like he'd just snorted some sulphate, but I'm pretty sure Lester never took any drugs. He always had them around, just never took them himself. Lester had to be in control.

Jonni and I used to meet up after work two or three times a week, always at his place. He didn't believe in going out much. He had a simple room, sort of monastic, really, and he kept a pinky-red curtain across the window, so the room always had a warm glow, except at night when he'd open the curtain and let the street light shine in. And Jonni would sit in the glow, red in the day, yellow at night, sit cross legged on his bed, and we'd smoke dope and drink tea and talk about stuff. We'd tell stories, kids' stuff, fantasies about living in ruined churches and riding horses at night through the forest, chasing the undead and the ghouls. That was when I wanted to hold him tight, but I never did. I always felt he might break.

Those were good times. Jonni used to talk about how people didn't get it at all, how they thought Goths were a miserable bunch, always depressed. They didn't understand that it's the bright shiny world outside that's depressing, the people who got their ideas on how to live from TV. Sometimes Jonni would play this little Indian harmonium and we'd make up songs. They were like hymns, funny hymns, about decay and darkness and slagging off all the things we hated. He made a song up all about Lester, who he called the Lizard. He hated Lester, but he never quite told me why. I didn't hate him. Lester wasn't a Goth at the time but I didn't mind it when he came round the shop. He made me laugh. I said this to Jonni once and he took my hand and said:

'You'll always be all right. You never really let the world get to you, do you?'

I didn't know what he meant at the time, and, just for a moment I felt like one of the reporters who came round the shop, asking what it was all about. Like he knew and I didn't. Then his eyes softened and he started singing another song. We never talked about Lester again after that.

Then one summer evening about two years ago, almost to the day, I called round as usual and he wasn't sitting on his bed, he was lying flat, his arms stretched out in the deep pink glow, perfectly still. I'd never seen him look so beautiful. His eyes were closed, his skin looked like marble.

I touched his forehead then quickly drew my hand away. It didn't feel like Jonni, it felt like cold meat.

Everyone thought he'd OD'd, but if he had, it was an accident because Jonni loved living. He was fine that day at work. No hint of anything bad in the air. There was a sort of family cover up and no one would tell us anything, so we never did find out. I took it quite badly, and I dealt with it by taking it out on Matty, who I just ignored, and Lester who I snapped at like he was an idiot whenever he asked me anything, like where stock was kept or why we priced things the way we did. It was a few days before I stopped crying.

It was me who urged Lester to take the first sip. He was playing around with the phial of blood, talking to it like it was Jonni, and I didn't like that.

'Now's the time, Lester. You've got to drink Jonni'.

I was still sure he wouldn't do it. He stood there for a moment and I thought he was about to cry or faint or something. Or yell out in horror. But it was nothing like that.

'Are you sure it's clean? I mean, you know, Jonni...'

'Yeah, it's fine. Jonni had the tests. Jonni was clean.' Which was true. If Jonni used needles I'm sure he didn't share them, he was a pretty solitary guy, and it was me who urged him to get tested. Maybe in the back of my mind I still thought one day me and him might get it together. And I was so low at that moment I thought fuck it, let's drink the blood even if it's bad, I'll just follow Jonni, to wherever Jonni's gone. That's how I felt then.

Lester looked at me - he didn't look at Matty, he just stared straight at me. It was like his brain was going through some heavy calculation, or he was working the flippers back and forth on a pinball machine until he got the ball just right. Then he got it; his eyes lit up and he gave a big flashing smile.

'Wow. That's so cool. A real homage to Jonni. And we'll be the only proper Goth shop, the only one run by real vampires.'

'Vampires,' said Matty, chewing on the word like it he had never tasted it before, 'Fucking vampires.'

'Hey now Lester, this is a private thing,' I said, still not thinking he was going to do it, 'I don't think we should tell anyone. Just between us and Jonni's ghost.'

Not that Jonni had a ghost. Not then.

'Oh, we won't have to tell anyone, trust me. But they'll know. Somehow they'll know.'

He uncorked the phial and poured it into a tablespoon. He took a sip then passed it on to us.

Looking back now I realise that Lester saw it as more than a weird little bonding ritual or a test of how Goth we could go. No, Lester saw it as a marketing strategy. And in a funny sort of way he was right.

The first time you drink blood it's weirdly familiar. I've tasted blood before of course, like at the dentist's or when I've cut my lip, but someone else's blood has a strange tang to it. It's got that standard milky texture and metallic edge, but then there's a shock, like you get when you pick up the wrong cup of tea and you get the one without sugar. I wish I could tell you it was more exciting than that, but it wasn't. We all had a taste of Jonni's blood then went home.

For the next week it was like we shared this dark secret. Maybe it was just in my head, but people seemed to be giving us weird looks; even the weird people were giving us weird looks. And I began to feel a little like Jonni myself. We were all slowing down. Not that there could have been enough smack in those few drops of his blood to have any effect, but I did feel like I was joining Jonni in some sort of heroin haze.

'Sympathetic endorphins' said Matty, 'like just a few molecules kicks something off in your own bloodstream. Chemical empathy. That's how homeopathy works.'

I knew he was talking shit, but it seemed the right sort of shit for that moment. I grabbed his hand and nodded. However half-baked his ideas, Matty was still one of us. This was the time when we were closest. Jonni had gone and Lester, well, Lester was there but it was like he was still arriving.

Something began to go wrong in the shop after that. Lots of people dropped in, more than ever, but they stared at us and then made a hasty exit. Maybe that vampire vibe was just far too strong, or probably it was just we weren't in the mood for selling any more. Matty was convinced that drinking Jonni had turned everything bad, but Lester just laughed and winked. Lester didn't seem too bothered with how things were going, but Matty knew. Matty did the books, Matty knew how much money we were losing. And it was he who spoke up first.

'This is all fucked up. We should never have drunk the blood. That was just fucking wrong.'

I nodded.

Lester thought for a moment. 'No', he said, 'it was the blood that was wrong.'

'The wrong blood? What the fuck is that supposed to mean?' I shouted. I really hated him at that point. Jonni was right, he was a grinning lizard.

'Don't you get it? It's too much of the Jonni vibe.'

'Everyone loved Jonni,' I said.

'Yeah, but we can't all be Jonni. Anyway, Jonni didn't sell'.

I didn't like the way Lester said that, like Jonni was part of the merchandise. But Jonni wasn't a salesman. Jonni hated selling, he'd always look guilty when a customer passed the cash over. And usually they didn't, they talked to Jonni; when they bought they bought from Matty or me.

No more was said over the next couple of weeks; the Jonni vibe gradually wore off and trade began to pick up. Matty cheered up; I have a feeling Lester had put some money into the business, bought a share or something, but Matty never said a word to me about it. I have to give it to Lester, he had a knack with the customers, particularly the younger tourist kids who would come in with their parents. Lester would chat up the Mums while the kids perused the racks. His trick was to make it feel like fancy dress to the parents, and something really secret and bad to the kids. He was brilliant at that. Like the parents never got the irony. That was impressive, for a Yank. Yeah, Lester could sell.

We had almost forgotten about the blood on the morning Lester came in and said:
'I found some. And it's really pure. You can't get purer than this.'
And held up this bag. This clear plastic hospital bag. Full of blood.
'Where the fuck did that come from?' I asked.
'We're not doing that any more,' said Matty.
'We did it before and we'll do it again. Because we're the real Goths. This is how we keep ahead.'
I thought to myself at the time, how could any real Goth make that statement? I thought it, but I didn't say it.
Matty said it probably wasn't real blood, or at least not human blood. And that began to freak me out. I'm vegetarian, you see. Lester just sniggered and said:
'It's real all right, and human. As pure as it can be. I'll show you.'
He took a sip first from this little brass cup then passed

it to us. Even then it seemed like a stupid thing to me, Lester getting it wrong again. I could have said no, but that would have been like letting Lester win that round, and I couldn't have taken seeing the smug expression on his face if we had turned it down.

It was Lester who brought in the white.

Everything we sold, everything in the shop more or less, was floor to ceiling black. Just a touch of blood red and dark purple. The only thing pale was our skins. Then one morning Lester said this stupid thing:

'The frocks don't look black enough.'

'What do you mean?' I said, 'They can't get blacker than that. They're black.'

'That's the problem - everything's black, so nothing looks that black. Like everything's relative.'

'Yeah,' nodded Matty.

'So,' continued Lester, 'To really look black you need some white.'

'Maybe he's right,' said Matty, 'relativity.'

And then Lester showed us what he'd bought. We never knew where he got it (we never knew where he got anything) but he took the lid off this white cardboard box, peeled away the tissue paper and there was the whitest dress you'd ever seen. Pure white satin, the wedding dress of a snow queen, with a tight laced-up bodice that sort of melted into this slinky stream. He put it on a half mannequin, just a torso thing, and hoisted it up to the ceiling. We stared at the shimmering object hanging above our heads. No one said anything for a minute or two. Then I broke the silence.

'No, that's not right. Bring it down.'

And he did. I scrabbled around in the back of the shop and found this necklace, jet black with a huge blood red fake ruby. I put it over the white dress, adjusted it so it looked like it was a sort of a bleeding heart, and Lester hoisted it up again. And you know what? Lester was right. Everything around it looked blacker than ever. As black as it could be. Then Lester looked straight at me, not at my tits but into my eyes, like this was the first time he'd really seen me and just said:

'Hey, you're really good.'

Matty went a bit sulky after that. He thought he was the one with the ideas.

Now I thought the white dress was just some display gimmick, to show off the other clothes. I didn't think anyone would want to buy the thing. But Lester had other ideas. The White Goth concept, of course, was all his. Matty and I thought it was a joke, but Lester managed to get all these kids to believe that the coolest thing of all for a Goth to do was to turn up to a Goth gathering dressed in white. It takes some guts, he would say, but it will be as cool as you can get. And it had to be cool; 300 quid cool. Yes, we all thought that was a joke too. Our customers, after all, were mostly kids, none of them had that sort of money. But somehow Lester built up this idea that this frock was so special, like it was the only one, and to wear it was like a prize for being daring. Of course it wasn't the only one, in fact Lester seemed to have an endless supply of them, and he never actually claimed they were one-offs. But there was only one at any time hanging in the shop.

That wasn't the only time Lester gave us that 'to look really black you need some white' line. Next he wanted to paint the walls. Yeah, he wanted to paint the walls white. Shiny white. Me and Matty laughed.

'We're not a fucking dairy,' said Matty, 'Not like we've gotta keep anything clean.'

'I was thinking,' said Lester, in a slow way, like he was taking the piss out of Matty, 'not so much a dairy. More of a slaughterhouse.' And then he laughed, and it was this hideous cackle. Not very Goth.

So shiny white it was. At least it wasn't tiles. We stayed up all night, with Lester getting us to sing all these old chain gang songs as we rollered the walls. I think the fumes from the paint got to us, because it became a party. Even Matty joined in; I'd never seen him so upbeat. I guess it was then I realised I actually liked Lester. He may have been a lizard, but he was a lizard who did things. You know how it is, you do something to get out of the routine, then that becomes the routine. It's easy to get stuck. Lester was good at moving on.

In the morning we brought the stock back in. God, did those frocks look black now. They didn't just look like dresses, more like deep holes you could lose yourself in.

And of course it worked. More people came into shop than ever, so many in fact that Lester had to vary the stock a bit. Our stuff had never been that cheap, or that well made. Probably made by people like us in some back room up north. So Lester started getting in cheap stuff from the Far East, T-shirts and trinkets and things, so all the tourists could go away with something. I even suggested to Lester he could get some 'My-Mum-went-to-the-Goth-shop-and-all-she-got-me-was-this-lousy-T-shirt' T-shirts run up. He actually took me seriously and thought about it for a minute or two before he said:

'No, baby. Not yet.'

I was surprised how excited Matty was when Lester bought him out, even though he'd talked about selling the place ever since it started. I thought he'd be a little sad, I thought he'd miss it but he just shrugged and muttered something about it not being the same any more. I think it was a relief to him he could stop pretending he had any idea how to run a business. He got to buy his cottage somewhere on a ley line where he could grow his dope and read the books he never quite understood. It's funny, but I didn't miss him. Lester gave him a good price, but nothing like the price Lester got when he sold the lease a few months later. I found that I didn't miss the shop either; Matty was right, it wasn't the same. Not since Jonni died. Anyway, we needed to expand.

You probably know our chain. It's cheap, very cheap, mass produced by kids in Cambodia or somewhere. It's so cheap everybody buys their stuff there. Not much Goth about it now apart from the tasteful little skull on the labels, but that's the way things go.

Lester and me. It surprised me more than anyone else. Lester helped me forget about Jonni, Lester never looks back. He looks to the future, and there's something so cool about that. And all the things I hated about Lester, his American smile, the way he bounced around, the way he saw everything as a business opportunity - they're all still there. It's just that I kind of grew to like them.

I asked him about the blood once, the stuff in the hospital bag, where it came from. He said he got it from the hospital on the military base where his father worked, and, yes, it was pure. Pure American blood. I don't know whether he was joking or not.

He was never really into the Goth thing, but maybe none of us were, not really, not deep down, only Jonni. I thought I was, I really did, back then I knew I was part of something special. I remember our last day in the shop, sweeping the floor and boxing up the last few relics of stock; a feeling that I'd lost something, but I couldn't quite get of hold of what it was. Like a trace of last night's dream.

And now, two years after Jonni's death, things have begun to change again. There's not much to complain about but

I feel sad these days, and tired. I stay at home while Lester works. I read a lot, and try to write stories, stories that meander everywhere and never quite end. But the good thing is those Gothy feelings, those dreams I felt I'd lost are beginning to come back.

Our apartment is big and new and looks down over the city. I keep the curtains closed in the day and open at night to let the street lights in. I roll myself a joint, and maybe chase a dragon or two, it helps me get through the day. I lie back on the bed and sometimes I hear horses neighing in the distance and these songs, sweet songs, echoing from a thin, whispery voice accompanied by a little Indian harmonium.

Sometimes I sing along too.

The Reckoning

By Nick Poole

There are 2 train stations, 12 different streets to walk down, 33 red doors, 17 bushes, 2 brick walls and 1 decorative chain on the journey from work to home.

Going home is not an option.

There are 2 newsagents, 1 chip shop and 3 pubs.

Right now, it is the pubs that interest me. Or 1 in particular.

I've always had a fond relationship with drink, but tonight it has the pull a choirboy has for my old parish priest. Work is shit, isn't it always? But home is...

I count my footsteps until the junction. 53.

Might as well stretch the elastic journey between work and home as far as it can go without snapping it.

I don't care if it does snap, actually.

There are 43 three paving stones and 2 drains currently full of wet leaves.

The Bullfrog was a regular haunt of mine, once. 23 faded red leather seats, worn through by 1,000 sweaty arses. 200 odd splintered wooden floorboards. 1 huge mirror behind the bar that adds exactly 0 extra light. I swear that's still Mad Doris talking to her cider by the quiz machine. Dartboard (1), carefully placed near the toilets to inconvenience both players and those needing a piss. Nicotine seeping out of the walls. Tiny television high up on the wall to ensure a cricked neck if you try to watch it.

All in all, a shining example of the British art of serving the customer.

At least it isn't home, though. Here, home is somewhere to worry about later.

"Professor! You haven't been in for a while! Where've you been?"

The publican, Martin. Greying handlebar moustache, hair dyed an extraordinary black. Calls me "professor" because I wear glasses and thinks it the height of humour. Probably is, in here.

"Pint of ESB," I say, perching myself on a high bar stool. 9% specific gravity. "And a whiskey chaser. A large one." Don't know about the Scotch.

He pulls the pint, and I watch it with anticipation. I know I'm here till drink-up time, now. Seems incredible that I should spend the next 5 hours sitting and getting pissed. 300 minutes. Sober, it seems a very long time to pass. I know tomorrow that it will seem like no time at all. If I can remember anything.

"What have you been up to, Prof? Heard you had a little girl."

It's like a kick in the heart. But how is he to know?

"Just get the drinks," I say. "No offence, but I'm not in the mood for a chat at the bar right now."

He gives me a quick look, maybe checking I am serious. Then he leaves me to the serious business of getting hammered. I start to count the optics and the bottles behind the bar. I count the Guinness bar towels and the Stella beer mats. I only count the beermats I can see without moving. There are 108.

He was right about the girl. 1 little girl.

3 fucking bastard years, that's all.

Actually, 40 months, 3 days and 2 months. I start to work out the seconds in my head.

"Same again?" Martin is already pulling another pint.

I wonder where the other one had gone. Then I go back to my reckoning.

*

When I wake, my mouth is full of sandpaper and my head is stuffed with wet dishcloths. Then I remember the other thing, and the hangover is not enough, not nearly enough. I start to count the heartbeats in my ears.

Five, six, seven, eight...

But I have to get out of bed because the heartbeats are not enough either.

I am still wearing the same shirt and tie from last night, now crumpled. The shirt looks as though I've had a nose bleed. The stairs are treacherous, but I count them all out, all fourteen, tentatively. My legs seem to be controlled in a different way than I remember.

The last step arrives sooner than I expect and I stagger against the front door.

The door to the living room is open.

Tanya is sitting in the middle of the carpet with pictures of Juliet surrounding her like petals from a rose. Hurriedly, I start to count the pictures, there's more than a dozen.

Probably thirty-odd. If I can be methodical, I won't double count.

Tanya looks up, red eyes accusing. I feel a surge of anger.

What do you want from me, anyway?

"I'm going to work," I say, the words croaking in my throat.

I know it is a lie even as I shut the front door.

*

I was angry with little Juliet sometimes. Yelled at her. Once I chucked her onto the bed unnecessarily hard during one of her tantrums, and shut the door on her screams. When she was a nearly a year old, I can remember wishing the responsibility away. To be done with it all, the whole being-a-father routine. Wanting the freedom to do what I wanted again.

You've got your wish, now, haven't you?

I am in the café drinking black coffee, counting how many sips a cup of coffee takes to drink and waiting for the pub to open. I had withdrawn cash with my credit card, something I never would have done once. How much is the interest? I try to remember the handling charges. I want to work out precisely how much thirty quid has cost me. But it doesn't seem important now whether I pay all the swindling cons the banks use to nick my money.

I smell like an unwashed beer glass smells when you pick it up the night after a party. I don't intend to get near enough to anybody for it to matter. If they come too close, that's their look-out.

I try to count the floor tiles, but the numbers keep getting mixed up with the number of times I sip the coffee.

"They can fuck off," I say aloud. The woman making sandwiches behind the counter looks up.

"Sorry, love?"

I stand up. Once round the park, and the pub would be opening. Not The Bullfrog, another pub. I don't think Martin will serve me again. I vaguely remember counting exactly seven thunks as I beat some smart-Alec's head against the door-frame of his pub.

I think somebody pulled me away. Probably Martin.

It explains the blood spatters on my shirt.

"I said," I raise my voice to a shout, "they can FUCK OFF."

I don't wait to hear her reply. I count my steps to the park.

*

The park is a mistake. The cricket green is all right. Nobody is on it at this time of day, anyway. No, it's what lies in wait at the far end.

The swing park.

Two swings, one see-saw, one roundabout, two slides and one climbing frame.

I count thirty-two dandelions as I walk. Two dried piles

of dog shit. There are seven trees marking the boundary to the houses and the river. Three benches. One old pavilion.

I should turn back, take the long way round via the river. It's not like I'm in a hurry. But I just carry on walking, and when I reach the red iron gate with its notice saying, "No dogs, please," I go in and sit down on the swing and listen to the chain complain about my weight.

I try to count the creaks, but now the numbers have slipped away completely. After a while, I start to cry.

*

Tanya is still sitting on the carpet when I get home. This time she doesn't even bother looking up when I enter the room.

I kneel down and wrap my arms round her.

"You've been a long time," she says in a tiny voice. I start to work out how long it has been, exactly, in hours, minutes and seconds. Then I let it go.

"Never mind," I say. "I'm home now."

Beer and Clothing in Hammersmith: An interview with the Ugly Sisters by Lester Kent

By Perry Iles

Beer and Clothing in Hammersmith: An interview with the Ugly Sisters by Lester Kent
Backbeat Magazine, Feb 2009

By 1979 Punk was as dead as Sid and Nancy. We were still two years away from the vapid horror of the New Romantics, and the charts were a talentless wasteland of no-hopers and novelty acts. Enter the Ugly Sisters. Their only Number One was She's So Fine - in fact it was their only chart success. Nine months later, they broke up as the career of one of their backing singers took off like a ground-to-air missile. So how have the Ugly Sisters filled the thirty-year gap since the hit? Fluffy Anderssen and Griselda Grimm – real-life twins Kath and Penny Turnbull - are now in their mid-fifties. Backbeat put on a helmet and flak jacket and went to the back room of an Essex pub to catch up with them last week. They're still draining the dregs of the dream – literally as well as metaphorically, going by the empty gin bottles. They strive to sound like they come from LA instead of Basildon. They still refer to each other by their stage names. But the job of a music journo is to take the rough with the smooth, and a musician's lot is not always a happy one. So pull up a chair and stand me a drink, and I'll tell you a fairytale. Once upon a time...

GRISELDA GRIMM: Yeah, it got bad pretty quick after *She's So Fine* went global.

LESTER KENT: How did it get so bad?

FLUFFY ANDERSSEN: Punk was, you know, tarnished, with the Pistols gone, and everyone saying how Sid killed Nancy...

LK: Well, he did, didn't he?

FA: Some say no. They found her in the bathroom. Sid was out cold in the bedroom, didn't remember doing it. Didn't remember not doing it either, so hey, bang to rights, know what I'm saying?

GG: The labels were churning out shit. Remember *Jilted John? My Perfect Cousin?*

FA: That was after us.

GG: Yeah, look what we paved the way for. *[laughs]*

LK: So what actually happened?

FA: The Ugly Sisters had been playing the punk circuits for a couple of years. We were good. I mean really good. We did the States...

GG: We did New York, Fluff...

FA: Yeah, OK, just New York. But we played with Iggy, the Ramones, the Dead Boys, Television, even Patti Smith once. McLaren tried to sign us, but after what he did with the Pistols, we told him to fuck off and went to the majors.

LK: And that was a mistake, was it?

FA: In spades, yeah. They thought if they gave us funny names we'd be big. It worked for the Pistols, didn't it? So they gave us names based on the old fairytales. Reckoned it lent us some kind of contrast with the punk sound, especially with us being real-life sisters too. Then they took doll's names and gave them to the backing singers.

LK: That was Sindie and Barbie, right?

GG: Yeah. Barbie used to dress up like the doll, but Mattel threatened to sue, so we changed her name to Barby with a Y and told her not to let her tits flop out of her stage gear quite so often, and they left us alone after that. Anyway, Barby left soon after and went off with some guy she'd met on the final tour. I think she just wanted to settle down and have babies. Last I heard she was living in Scotland, still with the same guy. Big family, good job, the whole bit.

LK: But obviously, it's the connection with Sindie that kept your profiles up.

FA: Sindie, yeah. That was her real name too of course, only it was C-I-N-D-Y. The guys in suits said no more backing singers after Barb fucked off, so we were left with just Cindy.

LK: Cindy says you weren't good to her.

GG: Well, yeah, we're not on her Christmas card list, let's put it that way. But she got a lot of mileage out of saying how bad we were, about the scene back then, all the drugs and shit. And of course, she stayed good looking too, which helps…

FA: Having a good surgeon helps too, yeah? Last time we saw her was at the Hall of Fame thing in '08, the night they were inducting her. Griz said did she want *us* in *her* backing band now, and Cindy said she'd rather power-drill her own head. Said it out of the corner of her mouth as she waved to the paps. Then she gave us both a huge hug so she could spark some bullshit rumour we were gonna reform. Face it, Lester, the only reason you're talking to us now is the past connection with Cindy, am I right?

LK: It has a bearing, yeah. Like Cindy getting put in the Hall of Fame has a bearing on *She's So Fine* being a top ten download thirty years on. Good to know that the old punk attitude isn't dead yet, though.

GG: No, Lester, it just went for a little lie down.

LK: Tell us more about those days with Cindy.

FA: Yeah? Like you'd want to talk about anything else, maybe? Sure you would. We toured for nearly a year after the single went platinum. We toured with old rockers past their sell-by dates and punk bands used to pulling bigger crowds. The record company sold us the idea. Said we'd have our own bus, and that was what got to Cindy. It was a proper tour bus, rooms and bunks, but there were only two rooms on it, and we had them because we were the band and Cindy was just the backing singer. She slept on a row of seats near the front, so it was always easier to tell her to get stuff...do stuff, you know. So OK, we bossed her about. She was only the backing singer - the hired help, yeah?

GG: We had this fairytale connection with the band's name, so with Barb gone we stopped Cindy wearing doll stuff and got her to wear rags on stage instead; smudge her face with dirt, backcomb her hair a bit, so on. That was us who thought that fuckin' idea up. Now of course the poster's everywhere. One of those...whassits? Iconic images? Like the cover of *London's Burning*, or that photo of Kurt Cobain crying. Anyway, while we were running about the stage making a racket and breaking stuff, we told Cindy to dress up like a bag-lady version of Stevie Nicks and do the backing vocals Julie Andrews-style. You know, all sweetness and light, eyes up to heaven and hands clasped in front of her. Gave us a contrast, a stage presence...

LK: A gimmick.

FA: Yeah, if you like.

LK: And it worked?

GG: Well it did for Cindy, obviously. 'Specially when she said *she* thought it up as a reflection of the way we treated her.

LK: That was the background. Tell us about the break-up.

FA: Hammersmith Odeon, the Rock Ball. New Year's Eve 1980. Why do you wanna hear it from us? You've got the Rock Legend already, why fuck with it? What's truth got to do with anything in this fuckin' business?

GG: Just tell him, Fluff.

LK: The Prince gig?

FA: Yeah, give the newsboy a big hand *[Claps sarcastically]*. That's the one. Prince, TAFKAP, Taffy, Squiggle or whatever he's calling himself these days. Of course, he wasn't big back then, but he had this quality about him, you know? He was four foot nothing, but he acted like he was six foot five. In the early days they were still trying to find a convenient heading to file him under. Couple of years later, they called it the Minneapolis Sound, but back then they called it punk-funk, so they put him on tours with punk bands and he'd wear pink leggings onstage and the crowds would chuck bottles of piss at him. Everyone had him down as a poncey little puddle-jumper, but of course he wasn't. He had this thing about backing singers even then; wanted to pluck them from obscurity, make them stars. Fuck 'em bandy as a kind of sideline, of course. He saw Cindy at the sound check. We went off to get ready, and he sent this manager guy for her while we were out.

GG: Oh shit, the manager! Huge black guy, camp as a pink tent, liked dressing up in ballgowns, that sort of thing. I guess Prince wanted the image again. Anyway, this seven-foot tranny came backstage and just took Cindy away. Said one of his boss's backing singers had come down with laryngitis and could she step in. Was she gonna say no? Like fuck she was. But she had no costume, nothing. She must have simpered a bit and done the Poor Me act, and this big guy gets her a limo. Probably the only stretch limo in London back then. Takes her shopping, buys her really expensive clothes so she could look good onstage, gets his makeup girls in, totally top to toe. Right down to these expensive glittery slippers. Must have been clear perspex or something.

FA: We came back from the bar, and we're like - where's Cindy? And someone says she's in Prince's dressing room. I went through, and there's this security guy on the door who won't let me in. And I can hear the band, they're singing, and I hear this voice and it's Cindy's. Not that she had to do a lot, just sing some *ooohs* and *aaahs* and look pretty. I say to this guy what's our singer doing in there? And he says she's not our singer any more, she's Prince's singer.

GG: So you hit him.

FA: Fuckin' right. What's a girl supposed to do? Well I tried, but he sort of grabbed me and pushed me away.

Anyway, we're seething, and when we go onstage we don't have backing vocals, and we're terrible, so two numbers in I take off my guitar and trash it into the drum kit, and we walk off to all this feedback and booing, and I thought let Prince's fuckin' road crew clear up the mess.

LK: So you had a few beers.

GG and FA: *[together, laughing]* Yeah, we had a few.

FA: We got pretty bombed. But it was just beer. Course, the Legend has it we were coked up, we were dusted, we'd taken a cocktail of speed and painkillers and topped it off with two pints of Jack Daniel's. But it was just a few beers, that's all. And Prince is onstage, and Cindy's there singing, and she's looking pretty good and feeling pleased with herself. There's this glow about her, know what I mean? Like if she was made of chocolate, she'd just eat herself right up. Come midnight the music stops and everyone's shouting the countdown to New Year. Prince does this big hold-the-phone act and introduces Cindy to the crowd and says she's done good, and they're clapping and giving it five-four-three-two-one... and she's looking all aw-shucks and we've got this great big fuck-off bowl of trifle we stole from the rider buffet backstage. Trifle on the rider, for fuck's sake, but that's Prince for you. We're in the wings and she's only ten feet away and they're all onstage counting the year in, and like I said, we were pissed and angry, so I turned to Griz and said shall I? and she said yeah, so I chucked it at Cindy. Direct hit. Custard, red jelly, cream all down her. Suddenly looks like an extra in a Cronenberg film. She runs off crying, so fast she's out of her shoes, and Prince is really hacked off, so he does his encore holding one of her stupid plastic slippers, and someone pours champagne into it and the silly little fucker drinks it, and next day the press is having a field day.

LK: But you were the band with the twisted fairytale thing.

FA: Yeah, they stole it all. The image, the ideas, the fuckin singer, the lot. Afterwards, we were nothing. Our fifteen minutes we're up, know what I'm saying? One of the inkies – *Sounds*, I think it was - staged a picture of Prince putting the shoe back on Cindy's foot. She's all dolled up and sitting on some posh chair that's been done up like a throne, he's the perfect gentleman kneeling at her feet, not like all these awful punk bands that swear on teatime telly. There's an insert picture of her onstage in rags, and the mainstream tabloids are all saying hallelujah, happy New Year, punk is dead. So that's his career into the stratosphere and hers with it. Plus the whole business helps fire off the New Romantic thing. Shit, we're to blame for Duran Duran and Spandau fucking Ballet too, I guess. And here we are, nearly thirty years on. She's in the Hall of Fame, he's got a different backing singer now, they're all rich and famous and we're here talking to you.

LK: I guess so. That's some really cool stuff. A great new slant on an old legend. Thanks, ladies.

FA: What, like, that's it? You don't want to know what we've been up to since then?

LK: Well, the main article's about Cindy, really. Thirty years on, Hall of Fame, Tussauds, so on. Your interview will go in a side slot, I'd imagine, but it doesn't mean our readership won't remember you. And the royalties from the single come because of Cindy, really, don't they? It's the connection thing. One song, thirty years ago, and you guys make as much out of it as Noddy Holder from chucking out Slade's Christmas song every year. The trade-off works, you have to admit it.

GG: Oh is that right? Well, fuck you pal.

At this point the Ugly Sisters terminate the interview and walk out. Somewhat unsteadily, if you'll forgive this reporter's observation. The years haven't been good to them; they've moved on from the sassy heyday punks they once were and they're starting to inhabit the mantle of their name. But at least the old punk attitude still survives in this quiet backwater of rural England - only now it wears high heels and orange make-up. Lester Kent brought you Fear and Loathing in the Boonies, risking life and limb in the wastelands beyond the M25 for your enlightenment and edification. You can all head back to the main article now...

Lotte's Rats

By Dan Holloway

LOTTE'S RATS

In 1933 the brilliant scientist Liselotte Fröhm carried out an experiment with rats. She showed that, if a dopamine precursor were administered at the right moment as few as four times, even without a food reward the rats could be trained to pull a lever ad infinitum, until eventually they died of starvation and exhaustion. If she had been less of an empiricist, or perhaps if she had been more of one, she might have recorded her observation that even when the dopamine reward was stopped the rats' beady little eyes seemed to film over and remain transfixed on the lever.

Unfortunately for Dr Fröhm, a colleague had discovered that the rats had been bred by a Jewish-owned company and all her records were destroyed. "No wonder the rats behaved so stupidly," her Professor, himself a Jew, berated her, "they're fucking Jewish rats."

Lotte spent the next six years working as a junior experimental psychologist for the pharmaceutical giant, Bayer, conducting experiments to determine by how much cough linctus could be diluted before people noticed that it didn't work. For a few months her old Professor, whose loud denouncement of her had so far kept him his job, was able to do enough for her from a distance to ensure that some of the results of her cough mixture experiments were published in university papers. But when the great purge came later that year and he lost his post, all outlets for her work dried up.

Unaware that the Professor had been pulling strings for her, Lotte worked with more and more diligence, used larger and larger sample groups and more and more controls. Still nothing was published, and one day in 1939, exhausted, she felt dizzy, sat down, and within a minute was dead from a massive heart attack.

A PARROT FEATHER

The colleague who orchestrated Lotte's downfall was Ilke Haneke. Ilke lacked Lotte's patient ability to carry out painstaking experiments and obtain flawless results, but had a theoretician's ability to keep one eye focused outside the lab, hooked up to the wider picture, and another eye that was tuned to the finest detail. Detail such as the provenance of a shipment of rats, tucked away in the corner of a consignment note where others might miss it. A wider picture in which an experiment with rats might be used to shape a woman's future.

Dr Haneke ordered another consignment of rats, far fewer than Lotte had used but the eye she kept on the wider picture told her that this was a trivial detail, from suppliers in England. She repeated the experiment on two groups of rats, with exactly the same results as Lotte had achieved. She wrote down every observation meticulously, concluding that, "even when no reward comes the rats' glassy little eyes stare as if in awe, as though their belief in the source of hope cannot be shaken even to the point of death."

Now Ilke is typing the last sentence in bold and repeating it, again in bold, on the title page of her notes, just below her name. She doesn't hand the notes to her Professor. He doesn't even know that she has carried on with Lotte's experiment. He is a Jew and his time is very nearly over. It is a shame because he is a brilliant man, but that is the way of things. People and structures change, and success must rely on transferable skills. So instead of taking her notes back to the lab, she places them in a folder she has made for the purpose, pours herself a drink, and lies on her bed until it is time for the party.

There is nothing in Ilke's bedroom except herself, and her intimacy with the finest details of her body and her mind. She can draw a map of the contours of her pleasure that is accurate to a watchmaker's tolerances. She can locate every one of her desires on the folding layers of her conscious and subconscious. Now she has her eyes closed and traces the heat of the brandy down her gullet and into her belly where it merges with something else, something that has risen up from her viscera, pre-sensual and semi-formed. Not a taste, not a scent, not even electricity arcing in the gap before touch. It is a friend she thinks of as das unheimlich heimlich, the uncanny familiar. We might call it the awareness of possibility. It is the feeling we get the moment before we open a letter from someone we have known all our lives. It looks just like every letter they have ever sent, but das unheimlich heimlich already knows that it is a proposal of marriage.

Now, as the knowledge that she is about to dress for a party percolates through her, das unheimlich heimlich nudges Ilke in the belly and throws her back into an arching spasm that opens her throat with an involuntary cry that could almost have been a laugh. She opens her eyes and once again she is in her room that is filled with nothing, only it no longer feels like an empty nothing but a nothing of infinite possibility.

She turns her head and sees, on her bedside table, the only thing that she keeps in her room: a sleek, tapering, petrol blue parrot feather. Like a mote of dust that seeds ice within a cloud, it is a mote of colour in her blackness, seeding the rich landscapes of her success. She reaches for it and with one hand she holds it lightly on the dip between her breasts, not an inch too high or an inch too low, and she arches her back and her throat opens and lets out an involuntary cry that could never be mistaken for a laugh.

ULLI SWIMMING IN CIRCLES

This is a moment, and moments should be seized. Ilke arranges the papers in the folder, so that the words typed in bold appear in the window she has cut, only slightly less centrally than her name. It is an unusual folder and she is not quite sure why she made it as she did; but the eye that she keeps on the wider picture picked out the patterns that she used as if it had caught the direction of the wind that dried it and made it blink.

The folder itself is made of plain cardboard, cut square with a window two thirds of the way up like any document wallet. She has covered the card with draftsman's paper that she has taken into the forest and held over the trunk of an oak, rubbing the pattern of its bark all over with a wax crayon. This gives the folder a rather ancient look, a little like velum only dark and not so easy to place. In the top right hand corner she has painted in oils a rose that is on the verge of blooming into flower. It is the shape and colour of the garnet that nestles in the hollow of her neck.

Looking at the folder, Ilke feels almost giddy at its mawkish sentimentality, but she knows that it is perfect for the moment. The bark of the oak and a rose on the verge of bloom – images that are old but not too obvious, that pluck with just the right frequency at the sentiment of the volkische heart.

Ulli had been a prodigious swimmer until a riding accident had weakened her hip and she could no longer compete. Once she decided to be an actress she spent longer training in the pool than ever. At occasions like this, organized by her wealthy parents, she wears a constant smile because she knows that her teeth have a natural symmetry that it is becoming harder and harder for the rest of her body to maintain.

Ulli's parents love her dearly, and although they are financiers they are glad to fill their parties with film makers and ugly women in the hope that the combination will work its alchemy for their daughter before it is too late.

Today they could almost burst with the anticipation of seeing Ulli's smile broaden when they introduce her to their special guest, the newly appointed Minister for Propaganda, who is looking for healthy German faces to fill his screens with perfect German smiles. Imagine their despair when across the pool the reflection of the sunlight on a garnet hits their eyes and draws them to the perfectly shaped breasts and flawless hips of Ilke Haneke. Ilke throws her head back and lets out an effortless laugh that flashes enough of her teeth for them to know that Ulli's last chance is lost. She will swim more and more, but her hip will teeter and finally fail, and she will spend her days swimming round and round in circles with her smile exposed like the baleen of a ridiculous whale.

Ulli loves Ilke dearly and has done since they were small girls. Not so much like a sister as the way that little girls love their ponies. She feels the delight of Ilke's success, and seeks out her company, both the intimate moments when they talk and she encourages her friend, and the public moments when people crowd around Ilke and kiss Ulli on the cheek, congratulating her on what a wonderful friend she has. So of course Ulli has invited her best friend. Even if she had known what a moment it would present, even if das unheimlich heimlich had nudged her in the belly, she would still have invited Ilke, although she will spend the rest of her life swimming in circles like a ridiculous whale.

THE SENTIMENTALIST BURSTS INTO FLOWER
Ilke has closed her eyes in her bedroom and practised the movements of social ease so many times that there is no longer any hint of effort in her limbs. She seems to dance through the beautiful gardens and around the pool with a glass of champagne in one hand and the folder tucked under her arm, and the smile never leaves her face even though all the men are middle-aged and fat, and all the women are ugly, and she can't imagine how much longer she can keep pirouetting amongst them before her tiresome friend discovers her and marches her off, lighting the way with that embarrassing fake smile.

As she turns the corner of the gazebo there is a kick in her belly as if something growing inside her has received its soul, and before she can wonder what it might be she sees him sitting in the shade of a canopy.

"Frau Schmidt, you must have a drink," Ilke insists, placing her glass into the palm of an elderly lady and beaming, before turning in one movement and arriving at the edge of the canopy with the folder in both hands.

This is a moment, and moments are to be seized, she is saying to herself, but it is not what she is thinking. She is thinking that the Minister's eyes have not moved once from the moment she caught sight of him, that they have remained fixed on the dip between her breasts where she was holding a parrot feather only hours before. Not an inch above, where the garnet glistens in the sun. Not an inch below, where the black silk sculpts her skin. He will not move his gaze. She cannot move hers.

"Herr Doktor Goebbels," she says, the pause so slight that it may have been an artful syncopation, "I have something that may interest you."

"Yes." Still his eyes don't move but Ilke feels the cold intelligence behind them. She knows that he has taken in the folder with its motifs of the bark and the rose, the bold type in its cutout window, every inch of her body, and what feels like every inch of her soul, but she has no idea which of them he means.

"Do you have a secretary I can leave this with?" she asks, holding out the folder.

"I will take it myself, Dr Haneke." Now she feels his eyes exploring her, but she knows that they have already taken her in, and that he is running them over her now so that she will be aware of their movement, but she is already aware and her eyes do not follow his, because in her head she has followed them everywhere they are going, and invited them further. "Is it true?"

"Is what true, Herr Doktor Goebbels?"

"Is it true that rats can stare as though they are actually in awe of something?"

"Yes, it is true."

"And in what way do they look in awe, Dr Haneke?"

"The angle of the head," she feels herself demonstrating the slight retraction of the neck and tilting upwards of the head, "movement gone from the eyes," she feels her eyes fixing themselves on his, "and almost a tremor that has nothing to do with weakness of the body."

"Almost a tremor," he repeats, brushing his hand on her throat as though he is examining the angle of her neck.

"Almost a tremor."

Two days later the call came from the Ministry of Propaganda. Not from Goebbels himself, but from a secretary. Ilke felt heat like brandy in her throat when she heard the playful young voice explain that "Joseph" would like to see her about a job conducting an experiment. She could hear the pitch rise in the secretary's voice as she said the word, "Joseph," and she imagined him tickling her back with a parrot feather as she spoke, but she wouldn't let annoyance show in her voice because this was the moment that she had to seize.

BARK

"What is it, liebe?" her father said, his eyes as wide as he could make them, as interested as a father could pretend to be in the random markings his daughter has made on an expensive piece of paper.

"It's the bark of the jatoba tree, Puppi. It doesn't grow in Germany," the little girl explained.

"But we have wonderful oaks in the forest. We can get a piece of real bark."

"I want real jatoba bark, Puppi. I don't want oak bark. Everyone has oaks."

On a trip to Vienna, Herr Haneke mentioned the incident to a friend who knew an explorer recently come back from Africa. The friend spoke to his friend, and several weeks later a package arrived addressed to Mädchen Ilke Haneke.

"Look at this!" her father said, his eyes wide in anticipation. "What can someone have sent for you, Liebe?"

The little girl tore at the package and all the while her father watched her, barely able to control his anticipation. Finally she ripped off the last piece of paper and saw the beautifully sawn piece of wood, with a shallow round of bark clinging to it like the rind of a würst. Ilke clapped her hands with delight. Her back arched and threw head back opening her throat that let out an involuntary cry of joy. She flung her arms around her father and showered his neck with kisses crying, "I love you, Puppi."

Herr Haneke's eyes filled with tears because he loved his daughter so much and he knew that he would give her anything she wanted as long as he lived.

THE EXPERIMENT

Goebbels explains to Ilke that he would like her to repeat her experiment with people. His eyes are barely still and she can sense the excitement in his voice. It is as though the thrilled modulations of his tone are feeding her, painting in the colours of her future. Over and over as he speaks she hears him repeating the same phrase, "think of the power this would give us".

It is unclear whether the "us" refers to Goebbels and the Führer, to the Ministry, or to the German people, but every time she hears it she imagines that it refers to her, to her and Joseph watching from a balcony as people dance for them without control. She sees herself looking down over the balcony with him into the pit and at first it gives her vertigo and then, as the voice repeats in her head, "the power", "the power", it makes her giddy but with hunger rather than fear and she has to make herself concentrate on what he is saying before she sighs, but that doesn't work because she still hears his voice, and she can feel a low moan rising in her throat and has to make herself cough.

For a while they talk about science and he listens as she explains to him about the effects of dopamine, and the things that may stimulate its production in the brain. He mentions possible chemical mass production and writes Bayer in a margin of his notes, but it is clear that what interests him more is investigating the way that human activity can release dopamine naturally in the brain.

She will have a house, he explains, a giant schloss in the country, divided into four, with observation windows for her into every room. She will encourage the subjects, who will also be divided into four groups, to carry out a task. Nothing special. Not something that they would naturally like to do, but not something they will hate. When they perform the task, each group will be rewarded with a different possible dopamine stimulator. One group will be given physical exercises of just the right level of exertion; the second will be put together and encouraged to cheer as a rousing scene is acted out before them; the third will be treated to recordings of the most stirring motivational speeches from the Führer himself; and the fourth will be stimulated to orgasm. After several rounds of task and reward, the subjects will carry on being given tasks and the rewards will stop.

"Think of the power this will give us if it works," Ilke says as she leaves, and feels every one of the points where spots of pleasure form as he smiles and his eyes follow her hungrily out of the room.

A HOUSE FULL OF WINDOWS

Ilke arrives at the schloss the day before the subjects. There are living quarters that she may use for the three months of the experiment that are three times the size of her apartment in München. She walks in bare feet so that she can feel the wood on her skin and imagines what it will be like when she owns a house of this size, and feels that it will not be very long until she knows. She places a few of her things in various rooms, but she leaves her bedroom bare except for a petrol-blue parrot feather on the bedside table that seeds the clouds of her future and creates rich tableaux on the empty walls around her.

For weeks the experiment goes well. Ilke sets each group the same task. She gives them a dresser that contains a woman's clothing and she asks them to take it to pieces and burn the contents – not demolish, that would interfere with the exercise reward group, but take it to pieces nail by nail and dovetail by dovetail, and pick apart the seams of every garment. Once the task is completed she gives each group its reward.

Everything she needs is provided for her by runners from the Ministry, and still there is no sign of Joseph. Ilke won't let herself believe that he has forgotten her. She knows how important the experiment is to him, and she remembers his eyes following her hungrily from the room, and the points of pleasure they brought to the surface of her skin that she feels them again already like the coloured contours of a map.

Finally it is time for Ilke to withdraw the rewards from the subjects of her experiment. The Daimler van pulls up as usual and two healthy looking youths take out the dresser, which they take to the speech rats, as Ilke calls them, the group rewarded with film of the Führer's most rousing rally speeches.

Ilke stands at the gallery window overlooking the large

room where piece by piece the ten citizens dismantle the dresser and every item of clothing it contains. She can see the way that from time to time they seem to be distracted from their task, flicking their eyes towards the giant screen where so far the film has appeared every time they have completed their task. She presses her hands firmer against the glass as the pile of cloth on the fire gets larger and the flame begins to catch. She feels the pressure fighting her back from the window and traces it through her arms and into her chest where it kicks and leaps and turns.

Think of the power this will give us his voice says over and over in her head as the cloth burns through, and she looks down at the figures dancing for her beneath them. She feels a giddiness at the height from which she is watching them, a giddiness that forms a chorus with the pressure building in her chest as the fire trickles away to nothing, and faces turn towards the screen on the wall.

"Look at the power you have." An iron strength presses her face to the glass and its cold sends ice into her stomach. Her back spasms and arches but its movement is checked.

"Look!" A hand thumps flat between her shoulder blades, forcing her chest into the glass. It releases her for a second until she feels weight tight against her, and his hand grabs for the front of her skirt forcing it up. Grasping for her in a frenzy until he finds her. The whole weight of his body pressing her to the glass. "Look at the power you have over them."

She looks and still they are dancing for her, staring bewildered and wondering why the light on the screen will not come on. She hears the rip of the fabric merge with the hunger in his breath. As he loosens his hold on her and enters her, she throws her head back and her throat opens to let out an involuntary cry.

"Look at them dance for us!" she screams. "Look at them dance!"

THE BLIND SPEECHMAKER

Three days later, when they have observed the reactions of the final group, Joseph leads her to her study and sits her down. The gloss from their lovemaking is still on her brow and she can feel his eyes watch as a bead of sweat disappears into the hollow at the top of her blouse. For several minutes she follows his eyes before he speaks.

"The experiment no longer needs you, Ilke," he says, "but I do."

Ilke is silent. She wants to finish the experiment because she knows what it would mean if it were a success. But she doesn't have the patience to care about the minutiae of endless repetitions. And she always has an eye on the bigger picture, which is moving on so quickly at the moment whilst she has stayed where she is for a month.

"I want you to come to Berlin and write speeches for me. Your experiment works. In this house you make the people dance. Now I want you to come to Berlin and make the nation dance."

The house in Berlin is vast, and it takes Ilke half an hour to pad in her bare feet through the room. Feeling the wood on her skin she thinks of trees and of the bark of the jatoba tree, of throwing her arms around her father and crying with delight.

It is vast, but within weeks she has filled it with things: exquisite and colourful things. If she sees something that intrigues her Joseph has it brought to her house and placed where she desires it; but she always leaves the bedroom empty.

It is night and the empty bedroom walls are blue in the moonlight. Earlier tonight Joseph has delivered the first of Ilke's speeches. It was not appropriate for her to be there, but as soon as it was over he came to her and relived the glorious reaction of the crowd as he made love to her. Now, as she lies alone, she feels a knot in her belly that she does not recognise. Das unheimlich heimlich is nudging her, and she turns her head and sees the parrot feather, bluer than ever before in the blue of the moonlight; from it she tries to seed the colours of her future into images on her bedroom walls.

But tonight the images won't come. She stops trying to make them because she knows that this is what das unheimlich heimlich is nudging her to say. It will never be appropriate for her to listen to the speeches. She is in her beautiful, vast house, and the whole nation is dancing outside.

ILKE'S LAUGH

The Professor runs his hand over Lotte's belly, drawing a wake in the smooth sheen of her skin. It seems to him as he studies her that she hasn't aged a day since he met her when she was a graduate student nineteen years before, and he wonders if she thinks the same of him.

"I want this moment to be repeated again and again for ever," Hans says to her, running his fingers again and again over the downy skin of her belly as if sympathetic magic might make it true.

"Things are perfect now," Lotte says back to him, "I could wish for nothing more than that they always stay the same."

They dress hurriedly. Lotte waits a minute or so after Hans had gone, and again it surprises her that she doesn't wonder when they might stop having to keep up the pretence. She has never wondered. Things are perfect as they are and she wishes for them always to be the same.

She arrives at the interview room several minutes after him and looks at the two candidates for the junior research position sitting outside. One is a young man whom Lotte thinks looks rather like the Bauhaus Modernist van der Rohe, the other a young woman who reminds her of Garbo.

As Hans and Lotte discuss the candidates' performance in great depth, wondering if they could ever work with a man who reminds them of Modernism, they look out of the window and see the two candidates exchanging pleasant conversation. The young man is pleased with himself because he has said something amusing, and the young woman's back arches effortlessly and she throws back her head and lets out an involuntary cry, that Lotte is sure is a laugh, with such insouciance Lotte and Hans know at once that they want to work with her, and to carry on working with her for the rest of their lives.

They go out to the waiting room and shake Ilke by the hand, congratulating her on her appointment. The three of them smile. Then they break into a giggle. The young Modernist sits confused, sure that he hasn't said anything quite that amusing. Lotte is so happy she laughs uncontrollably and she cannot imagine a time when the three of them won't be laughing together.

Insatiable

By Jane Dixon-Smith

Eleanor Moore sat next to her husband and watched Mrs Jenkins hammering on the piano keys; the voice of the middle-aged woman frayed the nerves of the guests. Eleanor could see Mr Jenkins' hand stroking Mrs Hardy's knee, and she marvelled that the singer was able to retain her composure. Her chest heaved as her voice rose even higher, as though the volume might somehow dissipate her spouse's poorly hidden advances.

Eleanor's husband leaned closer to her. She felt her skin tingle at his nearness.

'I'm afraid, my dear, that there are some letters to which I must attend.' He turned to Eleanor's mother. 'Mrs Whitely, would you be so courteous as to allow me the use of your study?'

'Yes, of course. Go right through,' Mrs Whitely said. 'It was my husband's favourite room, before he died. You should find everything you need. Bess is working in the room next door. Give her a call if there's anything else. She won't mind the interruption.' She flicked a hand toward a passing servant.

'I will not be long, my darling,' said Mr Moore, kissing Eleanor's hand.

'I pray that your correspondence will not keep you from me for long.'

Eleanor smiled at his back as Moore swept from the room.

She continued to stare long after he had left and absently twisted her wedding ring around her finger. She had been married but one day, and the band of gold still felt strange, uncomfortable. They were still enjoying their marriage celebrations at her mother's home, and would travel onward the following morning to Moore's establishment in London.

Mrs Jenkins' voice reached a new level. Eleanor could no longer class the sounds coming from her mother's guest as singing. No, it was something much less ... endurable.

Mrs Whitely leant toward Eleanor and said, 'Stop it, child!'

'Mother?'

'Fidgeting. It isn't seemly.'

Eleanor willed herself to relax, but the previous night remained at the forefront of her mind.

It had been her first time.

He peeled away her dress until she stood only in her undergarments. She shivered as he looked at her. His eyes wide with passion and desire ...

'I said, stop fidgeting,' Mrs Whitely snapped.

'Yes, mother.'

She avoided her mother's stare and looked instead at Mr Jenkins. He leaned closer to Mrs Hardy and whispered something. Mrs Hardy giggled. Eleanor glanced at Mrs Jenkins. The older woman's face had hardened. She stared ahead, her voice not quite as steady as it had been a few moments before.

Eleanor's thoughts slipped once more to her wedding night. To the way her husband had been so tender, the way he'd settled her nerves.

He slipped the shift from her shoulders. Naked, she looked up at him, her lips parted in fear and wonderment. He touched her shoulder and waited for a reaction. She flinched, then relaxed, and he took a step closer ...

Mrs Jenkins reached the highest note; thankfully it was the last. She pushed back her stool, gave a small bow, and the intimate audience applauded her effort. With a grim smile she strode across to Mr Jenkins, who removed his hand from Mrs Hardy's knee, sat up straight with a little cough, shuffled to one side and patted the couch next to him.

Never I, thought Eleanor.

She was young, but she had observed the same awkwardness in other marriages. They all seemed so distant with one another, passionless, stale. But she and Moore would never be so cold. No, there would always be warmth in their marriage. Always.

He ran his hand from her shoulder to her breasts. She gave a small gasp, and he smiled. He leaned forward and found her lips with his own. He took her bottom lip in his mouth and she melted, kissed him eagerly. He cupped her back and pulled her against him ...

'And how are you, my dear?'

'Pardon?'

'Wake up, girl. Mrs Jenkins asked how you are,' her mother snapped.

'I am very well, Mrs Jenkins. Thank you for asking.'

'A married woman, eh? You'll be on your own now, I suppose, Mrs Whitely? Just you and your eldest daughter? Or will your son be returning soon?'

On her own, Eleanor mused. Her mother had been on her own since her father passed away. She had retreated from society. Friendships that had once been so vibrant had now all but evaporated. Even tonight's soiree was something of a rarity, in honour of Eleanor's impeding departure to the city. Or perhaps it had been she who was alone. With her mother a virtual recluse, her sister, Grace, too ill to be in the company of others, and her brother, Edward, away, scraping an income to support them and repay his father's debts, Eleanor, too, had been alone. But now she had a husband. Older, yes. Considered by neighbours and friends to be a substitute for the affection her father had once bestowed. But he was still a man who had shown her more love and affection in one day than the rest of her family had in a twelvemonth. It was a mystery to her, how her relationship with her family had become so strained since her father's death.

'Mr Moore,' she said.
'You're so beautiful,' he replied. 'Your skin, your hair, your eyes.'
He stroked a lock from her face with hands that betrayed his age. She curved her back, pressing into him. He bent forward and kissed her again ...

With no other volunteers, Mrs Hardy sat before the piano, shuffled the sheets of music, and began to play. Mr and Mrs Jenkins sat beside one another, listening in stony silence.

Something occurred to Eleanor. What if her husband had intended that she follow him into the study? Perhaps he craved a private moment with her? Perhaps he could not wait to resume the passion of their wedding night? Or would she be disturbing him, delaying his return to her side still longer? Yes, she decided, he would think her a nuisance, and she cursed herself silently for such thoughts.

She tried to think of something else as she listened to Mrs Hardy's performance, but she simply couldn't. Her first experience of intimacy played on her mind and she was unable to concentrate on anything else. She shook her head, but nothing worked. She wanted Henry again, just like before.

She moaned as the desire heightened. She closed her eyes and he stroked her pale, innocent face. He kissed her again, fiercely, without restraint ...

Eleanor felt her heart beat faster. Her face grew hot and she ached with longing. Mrs Hardy attempted to outdo Mrs

Jenkins with her falsetto, but nothing of the rivalry between the two women could penetrate Eleanor's thoughts. Henry had been with her in a way she had never experienced, never imaged.

She bit her bottom lip, crossed her ankles and clenched her thighs together in order that the pulsating sensation she felt might diminish. Beyond misted glass, the stark garden had a crispness about it; clear skies and bare branches betrayed an oncoming frost.

He unbuttoned his trousers in a desperate frenzy. She clawed at him, teasing him with an enticing look ...

She wondered once more if her husband's wish had been for her to follow him to her father's study. Were her thoughts those of a child? But after last night, she had become a woman. She pushed the notion to the back of her mind. It was her desire that she go to the study, not his. She glanced out of the window once again in a futile attempt to find distraction. Two birds circled one another in the distant sky, but it was hard to make them out now the mist on the windows had thickened. As the fire crackled in the hearth, Mrs Hardy's voice reached a higher register, and Eleanor's thoughts dwelt on her wedding night, she found her seat in the music room increasingly confining.

She kissed him this time. She gave herself wholly. She had been nervous at first, not sure what was expected of her, not sure what to do, but now ...

Eleanor's breathing became faster as the pace of the music quickened. She touched her cheek and felt hot, moist skin. Embarrassed, she took out a handkerchief and dabbed her face.

'Mother.'

'Yes, Eleanor?'

'I'm going to walk in the garden for a moment.'

'But Mrs Hardy is not yet finished. And Mrs Jenkins wishes to play another tune for us.'

'I'm feeling slightly unwell, mother. If you don't mind?'

Mrs Whitely sighed. 'All right, but do not be long.'

'Yes, mother.'

He let out a breathy groan as he guided himself into her. She returned a gasp ...

In the hallway, a servant held Eleanor's cape for her, which she received gratefully and fastened around her neck. Outside, the cool air bit into her pale face and she lifted the hood, pushing her mousy curls forward across her cheeks. Her boots crunched on the frosting gravel as she walked along the far wall of the garden, her breath forming misty plumes and her nose growing cold.

Despite the chill, the fire inside her had not been extinguished. She could feel where Moore had been - she ached, she burned, with the memory of his touch.

He licked her face, more like an animal than a gentleman, and she threw her head back exposing her neck and chest ...

Eleanor sat on a stone bench on the far side of the garden. She looked at the house her parents had shared for so many years. She was excited by the prospect of leaving for London, of being with her husband, but she could not help feeling that she was somehow deserting what remained of her father, of her family, by allowing Mr Moore pride of place in her heart.

He bit her nipple as the longing between them intensified. She pulled him into her, insatiable ...

She missed her brother, too. Edward had been gone almost three months. He wrote often, sent money, but their friendship had dwindled long before as a result of her father's death. She thought again of Mr Moore, and how his age, his authority, made her feel safe and protected. Every one of his embraces was a small moment of bliss. And of course, his large estate meant she would never again have to worry about money. She wondered, now she was married, if her brother would return to live with her mother. Moore's money would help fund the family home and ensure that Grace remained in good health. They could afford the best possible physicians now. But she had sensed a certain bitter tone to Edward's letter of reply after she had written telling him of her upcoming nuptials. He was entitled to be considered the head of the house now, but Eleanor suspected her brother felt that the older and richer Mr Moore would intrude upon that position.

Both their bodies gleamed with sweat. They were part of one another now, so lost in the same moment ...

Moore had been a friend of the family since she was a girl. When the proposition came, her mother pushed her forward fervently saying her older sister was too ill to marry before her. Mr Moore was a handsome man, but Eleanor hadn't thought she would be able to love him. It had seemed so unlikely, the possibility that she would one day she might marry a man of her father's age.

She looked down at the ring on her finger and realised she had been twisting it again. She sighed with contentment.

She was on top of him now. He clutched her face between his hands and pushed his tongue into her mouth ...

Unable to bear the cold a moment longer, Eleanor stood

and continued to walk along the path leading back to the house. A faint breeze had picked up. The sun was no longer visible above the trees and a shadow had fallen across the estate. It would be dark soon, and Eleanor would be alone with her husband once more.

He pushed into her. Faster, fulfilling their appetite for one another ...

She could hear Mrs Hardy, or perhaps it was Mrs Jenkins, singing in tones ever more shrill, accompanied by viciously struck piano keys. She looked to the sky and smiled at the hilarity of their predicament, knowing that she and Henry would never become like them. Not after the way she had satisfied him.

She accompanied every satisfying thrust with an appreciative murmur ...

She reached the east corner of the house and walked along the front, smiling to herself.

Faster, harder ...

Eleanor passed the study window and wondered if Moore had finished writing his letters. She wasn't sure she could bear to sit for another moment in that room without him beside her.

She cried out ...

The sound of the piano reached a new level of volume and Eleanor wondered where Mr Jenkins' hand had wandered to by now. She picked her way between the shrubs and, as the high-pitched female voice filled the night air, peered through the small, misty pane of the study window.

Spent, Moore stood up and fastened his trousers. He plucked his jacket from the chair. Hearing a noise outside, he turned and saw Eleanor's face at the window. Grace hastily retrieved her dress from the floor, lifting it to cover her nakedness.

The Sum of Us

By Amanda Hodgkinson

When I saw the snow, and how it had settled, like a thick white blindfold over everything, I considered going back to sleep. Looking back, it's what I should have done. Matthew had opened the curtains before he left for work, so when I woke up, I lay there, gazing at the blue glow of a cold world, until my alarm went off. I got up, pulled on jeans and jumper and made breakfast for the boys, listening to them discussing the snowball fights they would have later in the day. I hurried them all into the car, drove our three eldest sons to school and dropped our youngest off at nursery.

I drove home, parked in the drive, ejected the Harry Potter CD we'd been listening to, reached into the glove compartment to put it away and a green cardboard folder fell out, spilling papers everywhere.

I spent quite a while, reaching behind and under the seats, gathering up old receipts and Matthew's work papers. A letter had slid into the footwell of the passenger seat and thought I recognised the handwriting as my own, but as I scanned the words, I realised it wasn't. I felt the cruel surprise of it like a punch to the belly. It was my sister's handwriting. I read and re-read the letter until the words turned blurry. I shut my eyes tight as if it might help me, as if I might be able to undo the day, pull it off like a pair of too-tight shoes and step barefoot right back into the happy ignorance of yesterday. Then I began to cry.

Now it occurs to me, hours later, as I walk through steadily falling snow towards the railway station, that I haven't been alone in years. Normally I have the boys with me, or Matthew, and for the last few years, my sister. Thinking about her makes me clumsy and my foot slips on a patch of ice. I spin into an arm waving dance step trying to keep upright, stupidly snatching at snowflakes as though they might anchor me. When I get my breath back, I look around like a cat that's taken a tumble and damaged its pride. My first thought is her. My heart is slamming against my ribs and despite the cold I'm burning hot. But I'm still upright. I'd like to tell her that. She may have brought me to my knees this morning but I didn't fall. I shove my hands in my pockets, tuck my chin down into the collar of my coat and walk on.

I was holding the letter, still sitting in the car when Doreen rapped her ring-heavy knuckles on the window and asked me to let her into the house.

'I'm sorry,' I said getting out of the car, hiding my teary face. 'There was a play on the radio. I just had to listen to the end of it.'

'I've got to get on,' puffed Doreen, her scarf, a plump snake of green rolling around her neck. 'Are you all right, Claire? You're peaky looking.'

I waved my hand. 'The radio. You know how I am. I cry at anything.'

We were in the hallway taking off our coats and I realised I couldn't help her tidy up. I put a foot on the stairs, steadied myself on the bannisters.

'You know what? I think I do feel a bit off-colour.'

Doreen frowned. 'I can't do the hoovering. My breathing is so bad my doctor thinks I shouldn't be here at all.'

She gave a demonstration of her bad breathing, even managing a bubbling, mucus-loaded cough. I was halfway up the stairs. I wanted to ask her why she bothered pretending to be a cleaner. The most she ever did was read the paper, drink my coffee and dust the dining room which nobody bloody well went into anyway.

'Well, you do what you can,' I said weakly.

'I'll take a ciggie break first,' she called up to me. 'Then I'll see what I can manage.'

I opened my bedroom door and slunk inside. 'That's

lovely. Thank you.'

Collapsed on the bed, I pulled the letter out and reread it. Every word hurt. My name was there, amongst Charlotte's declarations of desire for my husband.

Let's run away. Let's go somewhere where it can be just the two of us. Claire is stronger than you think. She doesn't need you like I do.

Had Matthew gone after her? I buried my head in my hands. No. No. It couldn't be. More likely she had worked her charm on him. He always said she was flakey, off kilter, unpredictable.

'Two failed marriages?' he'd say leaving a small silence and then adding darkly,

'Doesn't that tell you something?'

No, she had never been his type. Until now.

When I heard Doreen leaving and the front door bang shut, I got off the bed and went down to Matthew's office. I have never searched through his things before and I was about to give up when I found three more letters in the bottom of a filing cabinet.

The notes were addressed to 'my darling Matt' when nobody, not even his parents has ever called him Matt. The thing that bothered me most was the little drawings the notes were liberally sprinkled with. All three, like the one I found in the car, were decorated with love hearts. I thought Matthew hated that kind of sentimental nonsense. He didn't even like me putting a row of xs on his birthday cards.

That's why I decided I had to confront them. I knew where they would be, the restaurant where they ate lunch together every day, just a train ride away from our home. A whole world away from me.

The snow drifts across the main road into the town and I walk for ages without seeing a car. Nobody's out driving in this weather. In the station car park, the commuters' cars have been parked for hours and snow has covered them so that they all look alike, rows and rows of vague shapes, dumb and frozen. Matthew's car is there somewhere. He and my sister must have parked it in the dark before they took the 7am train together.

For the last two years, since she moved in with us, my sister has worked as a dental receptionist in the same town as our printing business. She doesn't earn much but living with us, she can save her money. I always thought I'd been generous letting her into my life. Now I realise I was just plain stupid.

I haven't been to the station for a long time. The building is still dirty Victorian red brick and inside the waiting room, the grey painted walls have the same gleam of dampness on them as I remembered. I buy a couple of Mars bars and a magazine in the station kiosk. The magazine has an article on cosmetic surgery in it and despite mine and Matthew's view that true beauty comes from within, I can't help but be fascinated. My sister had her breasts done when she was with her second husband and, while I normally would never admit it to her; they look fantastic compared to mine.

She was always the pretty one and my four boys have taken their toll on my body. I allow myself a few tears when I think of that. Right now the idea of going to sleep while cosmetic surgeons busy themselves with a touch of bodily housework, giving me skin fresh as new bed linen with tight corners and a steam ironed forehead is an attractive one.

Of course, Charlotte sees everything in black and white. She has always accused me of being too passive. Apparently I invite people to walk all over me. If she were the wronged wife, she would be screaming blue murder. She would be gloriously in the right and he, Matthew, would be mortally, sinfully wrong. She would have changed the locks on the house, gone out and bought a new dress and confronted Matthew and his *ladyfriend*. She'd have probably taken my children with her to witness the scene because what greater strength has a wronged woman then the presence of angelic offspring at her side.

While I am the mother of four handsome boys, she is childless and, although I would never normally say it out loud, since the fibroids, she is likely to remain so. I open a Mars bars and eat it in three mouthfuls. My sister would raise an eyebrow at my greediness. Well, I raise one at her barrenness.

I eat the other Mars bar just as quickly, then check my watch. It is now 11.30 am and I can see a silver lining in this terrible situation. It could have been worse. It could have happened on a weekend when we would all be rattling around at home. A big, pressure cooker Saturday when everyone's bored and tempers are ready to burst. As it is, the boys are safe while I figure out what to do. Sammy is the only one I wouldn't mind seeing right now. I'd love to snuggle him close to me and forget all this.

The other boys are dark haired like Matthew but Sammy has inherited his looks from my side of the family. Sammy is pale, a platinum blond. With his blue eyes he is like my sister and I were when we were kids.

Charlotte is fifteen minutes younger than me but she still tells everybody she was the first born. When we were kids, our mother said it didn't matter a jot what order we arrived in. It did to us. Charlotte always had to be first in everything. Everybody imagines twins are going to be alike. We're not. While I dreamed of us growing up and marrying another set of twins, she dreamed of leaving. She wanted to be unattached, separate. Unique.

I get on the train and feel suddenly tired. I try to read the magazine but with the steady movement of the carriage and its warm, stuffy interior, I let myself doze, glad to be able to forget things for a moment. When I wake I realise I've slept with the magazine pressed to my cheek and a model's glossy face is stuck to my lip. A mother with three young children sits opposite me. She is kind enough to point out I have the face of another woman hanging off me.

We pull into the station and I watch her struggling to get her children into their coats, eventually manoeuvring them through the doors like a wide berthed trawler pulling in its nets with difficulty. As a single woman without my normal fuss of children around me, I slip past her, like an eel through water, smooth and singular.

I was three months pregnant when Charlotte left home for university. Matthew was just going into business with his father. Everybody had expected me to be the one to go on and do a degree but I had a baby to look forward to.

She dropped out of Uni. in the first year. We weren't surprised. When Joseph was born, I wrote to her but she didn't write back. Five years later, she phoned to say she had married someone called Peter. I heard nothing from her for another five years and then, out of the blue, we got a wedding invite for her second marriage. Matthew said we shouldn't go but I insisted.

'I can't believe there are two of you,' her new husband told me when we met.

'It's incredible. Now which one of you is my wife? Remind me?'

I laughed. I liked being a twin again.

'I don't think they're that alike,' Matthew said, taking my arm.

'We're not,' said Charlotte and ruined the moment.

That marriage lasted three years. When my youngest son

Sammy, had just turned two, Charlotte moved in with us. I told her having her with me made me feel whole again. She said she just needed to get back on her feet.

The sky is dark and stormy in the seaside town where Matthew works and the snow is turning to icy sleet here. I browse the few shops that are open while I summon up the courage to go into the restaurant. I buy a postcard for something to do. A picture of a gothic house on a black cliff, the home of someone who was once famous for finding dinosaurs fossils on the nearby beach. I like the house with its turrets and towers. It looks like a fortress. I slip the card in my pocket and walk towards the restaurant.

Before I left the house this morning, I went into her bedroom. I looked at the framed photos of my boys on her dressing table, the pictures of holidays and cricket matches and swimming galas, lined up amongst her makeup and her hair brushes.

We were at the public swimming pools with the boys only last week. A woman came up to us and asked if we were twins.

'And are they all your children?' she said, pointing to Sammy and Joseph and Paul and Andrew, all splashing around in the pool. I looked at Charlotte.

'We have two boys each,' I said. Charlotte laughed then and so did I. The woman joined in. Of course she did. We knew she would. Identical twins make everybody happy.

It seemed all right to lie. I divided my sons up between us. I felt rich, full of family and home and, it seemed to me, with two failed marriages and no children of her own, Charlotte had nothing.

I cannot put things off any longer. I go into the restaurant and the waiters greet me with uncertain smiles. They know who I am. In the summer months I bring the boys here. I sit at a table and order fish soup.

At first I don't know what to do with my hands. I have never eaten in a restaurant on my own before. I busy myself with cutlery, pulling bread from the basket, topping up my glass of wine from the half bottle I ordered, but in between all that there is a lot of dead time. Time I would normally have filled with chat and a bit of gesturing, a hand waving excitedly when making a point, or catching a glass one of the boys had knocked over, or even, laying one hand steadily upon Matthew's. I find the best thing to do between mouthfuls is to stare at the plastic lobsters on the walls. I sit there, letting my eyes go hazy and wonder if I might be coming down with something. I am sure I have a temperature. I decide instead that this is what betrayal feels like. A bad dose of flu.

Matthew comes in and I put my hand to my chest to steady myself. I'm so scared now; I think I might pee myself. He hangs his coat up by the door and walks to a table by the window. He looks comfortable, plump, a big, wool-knit jumper of a man. I am almost out of my seat when a blast of cold air whisks at everybody's tablecloth and I realise the restaurant door is open.

She's standing there, the wind dancing round her coat. Her face scans the restaurant and she doesn't see me. I can't believe she doesn't see me. She notices Matthew and her face relaxes into a smile. Charlotte takes off her coat, hangs it over the back of the chair and bends to kiss him.

I laugh loudly. It's not a nice sound, more of a high pitched snort than a giggle. I don't mean to, it just shucks up my throat and out of my mouth before I can stop it. She turns to the sound, looking round as if someone has called her name. Matthew follows her gaze and there we are, my husband, my sister and me.

Look at us, I want to yell. Look at the three of us. What do we add up to? What do I add up to now?

I don't get a chance to speak because my sister is getting up from the table, banging her knees and knocking over her chair, grabbing at her coat like it's a bird about to fly away. And then she is pulling open the door and she's gone.

I cross the room and Matthew stands up. He looks sick and he's saying something but I can't hear him because the door is banging in the wind and snow is swirling into the restaurant in hesitant waves, unsure whether it belongs inside or out. I am aware that everyone is watching us. That they are all looking at me, a plump woman in jeans and an old duffle coat and asking themselves why I am crying and why that smartly dressed blonde, who looks like me but is not me, just ran out, leaving the door open when it's cold enough outside to freeze the heart of St Nicholas.

Matthew catches my wrist and I let him pull me outside into the biting cold. I feel something fracture inside me. A kind of snap, like the stem of a wine glass breaking and all my belief in my life falls out and is lost. I snatch my hands away from him. Matthew is yelling at me.

'I made a mistake. Please. Forgive me,' he says, time and again as though the stupid man thinks it will make a difference.

My sister, coat flapping, blonde hair blowing in the wind, is running along the quay. She always runs. For once, I too, would like to run. But in which direction? I turn my head to follow her progress. The grey sea travels faster than she can, slapping the seawall, sending spray into her path, the waves chasing her down. Maybe she'll fall. Maybe the waves will catch her by the ankle and pull her under. But I doubt it. She is too quick footed for that.

If you had asked me yesterday who I was, I would have told you I was the skewed mirror image of my athletic sister running in the other direction from me. Now I am cleaved, halved and separate. I push Matthew away from me and fall into a jog. There's an energy in me that surprises me and I begin to speed up. I am sprinting. I can hear Matthew behind me, calling me, asking me to stop.

And I will stop. I know I am not the kind of woman that has the stamina for running. Matthew catches up with me and I lurch to a halt, hands on knees, head down, lungs burning, trying to get my breath.

He wraps his arms round me but I shove him away, looking past him, to the small figure, alone at the end of the quay. She is just a dark shape in the grey sleet, vague to me now as an island out at sea. I watch her cross the road and disappear.

'She's gone,' I tell him.

And with this pain in my heart, I am not going anywhere. Like I said, I have never had the stamina for running. As far as I can see ahead of me, which is only the next few minutes at most, I cannot say more than that.

Tied
By JW Hicks

I know cold. Winter, rain, snow; hurting toes, dripping nose, shivers. Cold.

I know light. Day, sun; warm hands, running feet, smiling, happy. Light.

I know dark. Night, tiredness, sleep, dreams. And through the dark, a shining thread, holding, tying...me?

I know sleep. I know waking. I know.

I. Know. Me.

I... me... June; sad face, dark skin and treacle-toffee eyes. Another face, a rounder, pinker face... Mother.

Mother... 'Don't you call me Mother. Remember, call me Cherry. Always Cherry.'

Cherry's hair is yellow, curly like mine, but yellow where mine is black. She has blue eyes, and she buys her curls. I was born with mine and born curls, frizzy curls are bad.

***

Sound, now there is sound. I remember sound, music, singing, talking, the beat of hand on flesh. This sound, though, this sound is snuffling, this sound is digging. I know this sound. A brown and white dog digs into a small dark hole, the dog backs out teeth clamped on a squealing wriggler. A hard quick shake settles the wriggling, silences the squeal and another rat is added to the pile. Scruff barks.

'Why's Scruff barking, Grampa?'

'He's counting, Juney. Going for champion ratter, he is.'

Grampa stretches above me, an oak tree. Arms as strong as branches, my grampa. He carries hay-bales, weaners, carries me. He combs my hair, gently like I'm a curly lamb. He counts the piglets one, two, three. 'Got to learn your numbers Juney. If you want to be a farmer, like your old Grampa.'

He taught me to read words, my Grampa, that summer I lived on the farm. The summer Cherry was working in a Blackpool show. He gave me books belonging to Cherry Scott, and he'd read me stories Cherry never told me, and how to write my name, June Scott, all neat and nice.

We had breakfast every day, eggs and toast and warm fresh milk. I'd help him clean the kitchen and we'd sing songs. I'd help him scrape muck or pick sweet raspberries and I'd wear my new black wellies.

According to Grampa people could do anything they wanted if they worked hard. 'Laziness is the biggest sin, Juney-girl. And easy-got money is the devil's treat. Me and your gran worked hard all our lives and were content... unlike some others.'

According to Cherry, farms were dead holes and the city was the only place to be.

I came in from the barn with the ginger kitten. He was my favourite, I called him Tiger and he was the biggest of the barn kittens. Grampa was talking on the phone, and by the way he set his mouth, the way he frowned, I knew it was Cherry on the phone.

'When?' he said, and after the phone squawked again he closed his eyes and carefully laid the receiver down.

'Cherry's coming for you early this afternoon. Straight after dinner.'

'Will she stay?'

'No, luvvy, she's just collecting you. She can't stop.'

'Can I take Tiger back with me?'

'You'll have to ask Cherry 'bout that, won't you?'

Cherry said they didn't allow pets in Family Care flats.

Grampa gave me a coral bracelet to wear. 'Your grandmother's,' he said.

'You can't give her that, it's too good,' Cherry said.

But he did.

***

The light is spreading and my knees are cold. Winter mornings, and me first up. Stale milk, a broken fridge and corn flakes spilled on dirty tiles, and me hungry for hens eggs and warm fresh milk.

More light…legs. Legs: running in new wellies, splashing in puddles, laughing. Now toes: cold feet pinched in charity-shop shoes. Late for school. 'Walk faster, June, why can't you? I'll get the nagging if you're late. Always the mother's fault, never the fucking kid's.'

'My toes hurt.'

'Always moaning, you. Your toes don't hurt. Only got the bastard shoes yesterday.'

'Don't know what's the matter with her, Miss Thompson. Reckon she's sickening for something. Anything going round? Losing weight? You think so? Can't understand it. She eats like a horse at home. I'll take her to the clinic. Could be worms, I suppose. She's always playing in the dirt.'

***

More light, growing light and barking, not snuffling. Is it Scruff? Has Grampa come for me? I miss him tucking me in, miss the warm quilt, miss the music he played on his old piano. He taught me nursery rhymes and counting songs. He liked me to sing, but Cherry says 'Shut it, you're doing my head in.' Miss Thompson liked my songs, she had me sing in Class Assembly, but Cherry couldn't come, she had to go somewhere else.

***

Words. I know those words. Swearwords: fuck off, shitting bastard kid, stinking fuck-hole cunt. They don't allow words like that in school. Miss Thompson told on me to Mrs Hunter and Mrs Hunter called Cherry in to see her. Cherry said she'd wash my mouth with soap, but she laughed as we walked home.

***

It's quiet. No more swearing, no more barking, no more scrabbling, just the shush of tree-leaves, the brush of grass and the twitter of far-away birds. I can't see the trees or the grass but I know they're there. The pale cord is also there. It tugs, I move; we're joined.

***

Sean O'Conner was one of the nice ones. Cherry brought him home from the place where she worked in the evening and he gave me a chocolate bar, and made me egg-toast for breakfast.

'She's June,' Cherry said, like she always did. 'My sister's girl. I'm looking after her while Diane's in hospital.' Then she paused and whispered, 'Diane's got mental problems.'

Before Sean came to live with us, I had to go to Mrs Pouter's for my tea and then she was supposed to put me to bed and look in on me till Cherry came back. Mrs Pouter was always shouting at her kids and they were always shouting back, so I did for myself like Grampa taught me. I made toast and cocoa and sang myself to sleep and Mrs Pouter never noticed.

After Sean moved in, Cherry gave up working in the club.

Sean bought me Clarks shoes that fitted me just right, and a new red duffle-coat. Most nights before Sean and Cherry went out, Sean would cook me fish fingers or sausages for my tea and then I'd go to bed. He'd say night, night June and tuck me in like Grampa. I liked Sean O'Conner.

Saturday. No school. A letter coming when I was eating my dippy egg and soldiers.

'Who's that from, Sean?'

'It's a job offer, darlin'.'

'A job? When d'you apply for that?'

'Couple of months back. Before we met.'

'What kind of job is it, then?'

'Manager. Scale three with prospects.'

'Good money?'

'Prime, and a Company flat. You coming?'

'Us?'

'No, you. It's time your sister looked after her own kid. You've been put on for far too long. I know, I know, she's a nice kid, but we deserve a life of our own, don't we? It's not like you've adopted her, or anything, is it?'

'Tell me more about this job, Sean. No, hold on. June, go play outside. Yes, you have finished. Get.'

***

'Where's Sean, Cherry?'

'Dublin. He's getting the new flat fixed .'

'He's going to live somewhere else?'

'Yeah, no, well he might be.'

'I like Sean.'

'Yeah, so do I. Now put that coat on, and do those toggles up. We're going out.'

'Where we going?'

'To the train station.'

'But it's dark.'

'Trains do run in the dark, you know.'

'We're going on a train? To Dublin to see Sean?'

'No... We're going to see Grampa... about a kitten. Hey, where are you going? I told you to put your coat on.'

'Got to pack if I'm going to Grampa's.'
'There's no need, no point. We're coming back tomorrow. And if you don't put a spurt on, we'll miss the train.'
'But...'
'One more word out of you and there'll be no damn kitten. Okay?'

***

Below the light is steady and the pale cord though shadowy, is still there, still linked to me. A gust of wind sets it into waving motion, it tugs me down and down, closer to the light, closer to the sound of trees.

***

The train wheels drummed, the engine whooshed and a whistle screamed. I sat close to the window looking into the dark thinking of Grampa and the tiger kitten.

When I stayed with him, I slept in a small white bed with a pretty quilt spread over it.

'Your gran made that. Cut the patches from old dresses and curtains. Always sewing, your gran. Not a lazy bone in her body.'

He'd leave the small square window open a little way. 'So you get used to the sounds of the country,' he'd say. He gave me a nature book and showed me all the animals that came out at night. 'This is how the owls hoot,' he'd go, making a hooting noise. 'And this is a tom-cat, yowling, this a queen calling for a mate, and this is a vixen's bark-cry.'

I was never once frightened on the farm. Not like in the flat. Not like in the city.

***

What's that noise? A whistle? Yes, like when Grampa's friend Farmer Berry sends Floss to round up the sheep. And that's barking. Floss? Or has the snuffling dog come back?

A man's voice, not Farmer Berry's, but a teachery, bossman. 'Hold the dog, sir. Keep back, please. By that tree, you say?' A pause, then 'Sergeant? Under that oak.'

More light, it's spreading fast now and the cord's much plainer, snaking down to a brown earth patch where gloved hands move leaves, dig soil, pick up small brown things.

'Sir?'

'Found something?'

'A leg bone. Looks like a child's. And there's this, sir. A coral bracelet.'

***

Movement. The cord, a dark strong line, pulls me with it.

The movement stops. Above me bright ceiling lights, picking out the line that links me to dark bones on a white table - a set of bones, placed like a skeleton - a small skeleton. Close by, on a white tray are scraps of red material, the toggles from a duffle-coat and a pair of Clarks buckled up shoes. Below the bones, on a square steel tray is a coral bracelet, the pinky beads linked with darkened bars.

I know that bracelet. When I wore it I kept those bars silver bright. There's a lady staring down at it. I know that lady.

Cherry's hair isn't yellow and curly any more. It is old lady grey and falls neatly about her face. Instead of bright red lips and blued lids she's pale and pink and... sort of grand. With her looser skin, thinned lips and wrinkled neck, she's got the face from Grampa's photo album, the face of my grandmother. But her eyes are Cherry's eyes, hard and bright and shining blue.

I look at her hands, gripped tight together as she stares. Those are Cherry's hands, gripped like they gripped my neck, that night in the dark under the oak tree.

And when she speaks, in her new soft voice, her careful, careful words, I still hear Cherry... my mother. Her voice is always with me.

'You weigh me down. You hold me back. I hate the bloody sight of you.'

'She's wicked, Miss Thompson. She's a liar born. Me hard on her? Me? You don't know what I have to put up with.'

I answered a phone call once, it was from a Mr Berry, and it sounded like Grampa's friend. He said he had bad news, but Cherry told me it was a wrong number.

***

'Sean, I been thinking. You're right. It's time she goes back to Diane. She's out of hospital and living back home with Dad. June? June's fine about it. She wants to live with her mother.'

***

It's the boss-voice now, the teacher's telling-off voice.

'Do you recognise this bracelet, Mrs O'Conner?'

'Yes.'

'We have ascertained, using dental records, that these are the remains of your daughter June Scott, who was reported missing on Sunday the 16th of October 1966.'

'Oh.'

'Will you accompany PC Daniels into Interview Room 3? Just some routine questions, Mrs O'Conner. Won't keep you long.'

***

'Before we start I'd like you to listen to this recording. Sergeant?'

And it's Cherry's voice, on the tape recorder, sounding as it used to, sounding harsh and cold. 'You don't know what she's like officer. Always running away. Soon as I take my eyes off her, she's gone. I'm always out looking for her. Reported? No. Those other times I found her quick enough.'

'When did you last see your daughter?'

'After tea, last night. She went outside to play. I called her to come in for her bath and she was gone, nowhere in sight. I was all night looking for her.'

'Did you not think to call us sooner, Mrs Scott?'

'Ms Scott. It's Ms. Shit, I was out looking for her. Kept expecting to find her round the next corner, didn't I?'

'That's enough, Sergeant. Turn it off.'

A long pause. Cherry fidgets.

'Mrs O'Conner, an eye witness has come forward to report a sighting of you and your daughter on Conway Road Station, on Saturday 30th July 1966. You were reported as boarding 8.30 train to Wellbury. On further investigation another witness, a ticket collector, remembers seeing you returning early the following morning...alone. Is there anything you would like to say with regards to these witness statements?

***

...In sure and certain hope of the resurrection. Amen.

The pale cord looses me. I rise, my wait over, and Grampa's calling me home.

Nothing Changed

By Derek Duggan

It's simple. The phone has a home. It's called a cradle. It's where the phone lives when you're not using it. It's where it gets its sustenance. Leave it off the cradle long enough and it dies. So, use it and put it back. At the very least, leave it somewhere it can be seen. That does not include among the remote controls. Or in the laundry basket. Or in the bag that she takes to work. Then I wouldn't have to play Hunt-The-Phone every morning after Bea leaves.

It's a small cross to bear; but it's mine. I would simply phone her to ask where it is, but, well, you can see the problem there. And if I'd known twenty five years ago that the beautiful girl carrying the heavy bags would annoy me every day with her lost phone antics would it have stopped me from offering to carry her shopping? No, of course not. Looking for the phone every day is a small price to pay for all that she's given me.

And I wanted to phone her. Something odd had happened. Something exciting. Something inexplicable. The water had disappeared. All of it. I had placed it in the chamber, set the timer and pushed start. Within ten seconds, it was gone. It didn't evaporate. It didn't leak out. The casing had maintained its integrity. It was simply, inexplicably, gone.

All I needed to do now was to figure out where it had gone to and I would be one step closer to home cold fusion. Affordable power for all. An end to the energy crisis. The end of oil wars, pollution, and not knowing where to look when buying your petrol from Mrs. Greene in the local petrol station. Why hasn't she had that fixed? One eye looking at you and the other looking for you.

I did two laps of the house, but no joy and no phone. I flicked on the TV, hoping if I distracted myself for a few minutes the solution would come at me from the ether. There was an old episode of Friends on. It was the one where Ross has the leather trousers and he makes a fool of himself while on a date. And that's when the next unexpected thing happened. One moment I was sitting, half watching the telly, half daydreaming, and the next I was holding the note. I looked at it. A single piece of paper folded in two with – Jack, on the couch, watching Friends – written on the outside in my handwriting. I turned it over, trying to remember where I had gotten it. I began to worry that maybe I'd nodded off for a moment and picked it up in my sleep.

I opened it.

Jack, it's me, Jack. Or rather, it's you, Jack. But in about ten minutes. Listen, I know what happened to the water. It goes into the past. It time travels. Can you believe it? So, I'm sending this note back to see if I can predetermine where stuff will end up. And I already know that I can because you're holding the note. This is incredible. I would phone Bea to let her know, but I still can't find the phone. But not to worry. Get down to the basement and get working.

Jack

It was obviously a joke. Very clever, but a joke nonetheless. And yet a glimmer of hope at the back of my mind drove me to pick up a piece of paper and write out the same words to see how they matched.

It was an exact match. Absolutely spot on, which was exciting, but also a little unnerving. I decided to prove to myself conclusively that it was a hoax. I scribbled an extra line on the end.

THIS IS NOT A HOAX.

I folded the new note over, addressed it and with a trembling hand, placed it in the chamber. I set the timer for ten seconds and pushed start. There were no flashes, no explosions, and Huey Lewis And The News didn't provide a soundtrack. It was simply there one moment, and gone the next.

And it had worked. I held the proof in my hands. Even the way I'd written the last sentence in block capitals seemed to be precisely the same. I wanted to share this incredible development with Bea. If only I knew where the phone was. If only she could remember to put it back where it belongs when she was finished with it. If only I had some way of making her understand that one day it would be really important for me to know where the phone was.

But, of course, I did have a way. I had a time machine. I could send myself a note yesterday and make sure that I kept track of where she left it. Except, I knew that wouldn't work because then I'd already have the note, wouldn't I?

I decided on an altogether more elegant plan, one that would nip the problem in the bud and sort it out once and for all. I would send a note back to Bea just before I met her. I was sure it would appeal to her romantic nature, sending a love note back through time, while at the same time ensuring that I would be able to find the bloody phone when I needed it.

I picked up a fresh sheet of paper.

Dearest Bea,
This might seem a little hard to believe right now, but this is a note from the future. Honestly. And I am your husband. You are going to meet me in about five minutes. I'm the awkward young man who offers to carry your bags. You'll accept and we'll hit it off straight away. Within the hour we'll be making love on the pile of dry cleaning your flatmate left on the floor. And I'll know from the moment I first touch you that we'll be together forever. You will complete me. I will live every day happy knowing that I get to spend it with you. You are my

goddess, my everything.

Just one thing – in our life together, try and remember to put the phone back on its cradle. Otherwise you'll drive me mental.
All my love,
Jack

I folded it in half and wrote – Beautiful Bea, carrying heavy bags up Aungier Street, five minutes before she met me – on the flap. I placed the little note in the chamber, closed the door and set the ten second timer. My finger hovered over the start button. In a moment I would know where the phone was. I focused, watching to see if I could identify the exact moment when things would change. I was particularly keen to see if there was any physical sensation connected with it.

I pressed the button. The timer began to click backwards. I watched the note and carefully monitored myself. The timer hit zero and the note disappeared. I didn't feel anything.

Nothing had changed.

I still had no one to call. That's the downside of living a semi reclusive bachelor life – you have nobody to share those Eureka moments with. Then again, you can walk around in your underwear all day. And you can wear the same pair of jocks all week without fear of anyone moaning at you. I sometimes think I'll meet that special someone; but you've got to be careful. I once offered to carry a girl's bags for her and ended up with a restraining order against me. And I was compelled to go for psychological evaluation, which wasn't a bundle of laughs, I can tell you. So, on balance, maybe I'm better off without people like that in my life.

I went back up to the living room to confirm my conclusion. Everything was just as I'd left it. The telly was still showing Friends, the dishes from my last three meals still sat unwashed in the kitchen sink, and the phone was still in its cradle, exactly where I left it. A pair of flies chased each other around the sink. Ah, for the life of a fly.

I did a quick computer search to confirm that I was still on the police register. I was. Nothing had changed.

I went back down to the basement. Maybe I needed to think bigger. Sending notes to random strangers was just too small. Perhaps my note had an effect but I just couldn't see it. I needed a more significant event, something I could observe, something that would be immediately apparent.

There's no point going big in half measures. You can't go half big. It's either big or it's not. And so I made my decision – Julius Caesar. I could send a message back and stop him being assassinated. Simple.

I picked up a fresh sheet of paper.

Hail Caesar.
You've got to watch out for Brutus and Cassius and a whole bunch of others. They mean to kill you, right in the senate. Question Brutus and I'm sure he will crack.
To your very good health, sir,
Mercury, messenger of the Gods.

I was pleased with this last stroke of genius. That was bound to get his attention. I folded the piece of paper and placed it in the chamber. I was just about to close the door when I realised that Julius wouldn't be able to read English. I retrieved it and ran the whole lot through an online translator. It gave me this.

Hail Caesar.
You've got ut vigilo sicco pro Ferinus quod Cassius quod a universus bunch of alius. They vilis neco vos , vox in orchestra. Question Ferinus quod I'm certus is mos fragor.
Ut vestri valde valetudo sir,
Mercury, messanger superum.

It would have to do. In fairness, he was quite a clever bloke so he'd be able to work it out. I copied the new message onto a fresh piece of paper and folded it in half. I wrote – Julius Caesar, the day before the ides of March, Roman Senate – on the flap. I placed it in the chamber, set the timer for ten seconds and hit the start button. I kept one eye on the timer, and one on the note. I heard the clockwork mechanism in the timer clicking down. I blinked and it was gone. I waited, then glanced around the lab.

Nothing had changed.

All in all this was becoming quite disappointing. I hitched the bottom of my toga up so I could climb the steps out of the basement. I was running out of ideas. I was sure there was some application for my discovery. I flicked on the home-amphi, hoping if I distracted myself for a few moments the solution would surprise me like a lion on a Christian. There was an old episode of Amici on. It was the one where Rossicus finds the slave hiding in the bath house and they all kick him to death. They say it's the funniest episode, but I don't know.

And then it hit me. I could use the machine to right the greatest wrong in the entire history of the Empire. I immediately lit some incense and placed it on my altar to Mars. I remembered that time when the Saxon, Richard Dawkins, said that you may as well pray to Maltesers as pray to Mars. His execution though; now that really was funny. Even thinking of it now brings a smile to my lips – the way he kept screaming No, no! I am simply here to debate! Oh, they don't make them like Beadle's About anymore.

My new plan was simple and would hopefully erase the shameful Hiroshima event from history. During the East War II, Rome had commanded that an atomic bomb be dropped on the citizens of that Japanese City. Cs of Ms died in the blast, and Ms more afterwards. I would write a note to the Governors of Hiroshima telling them to evacuate before the bomb was dropped.

I picked up a fresh sheet of paper.

Leaders of Hiroshima,
The Roman Empire stands awaiting the command of the Emperor. At his word, they will unleash hell. They intend to drop an atomic bomb on your city. All will perish. Evacuate at once.
A friend.

I felt, to avoid confusion, and in recognition of the possibility that there may not be anyone there who spoke the Gods own Latin, I should use my personal reckoner and translate the note into the now dead language of Japanese. This is what it gave me.

広島の指導者、

ローマ帝国皇帝のコマンドを待っている。自分の言葉では、地獄を放つだろう。彼らはあなたの街に原子爆弾を投下するつもりです。すべて消滅する。一度に避難させた。

友人。

Let's face it, I'd just have to trust that it was close enough for them to understand. There was a lot on the line here, but this was as much as I could do. I folded the paper in two and carefully wrote – *Leaders of Hiroshima, day before the bomb, Government buildings* – on the flap. I carefully placed it in the chamber and shut the door. I turned the timer to X seconds and, asking Mercury to guide the note to the right hands, I hit the start button. I watched the timer click back to I and then the paper disappeared. I waited. I glanced around the lab.

Nothing had changed.
There was still just me. Wearily I climbed the stairs and went to the window. Still a wasteland. It looked as though I had been unsuccessful in my attempts to stop the Last War. For all I knew I was the last living human on the face of the Earth. Perhaps, I reflected, the machine didn't really work at all, and the note I'd apparently sent to myself had merely been a trick of wishful thinking.

I shuffled over to the couch and put on a video. It was 友人. It was the one where ロッス pretends that he used to be Sumo. It's very funny. But then again, it's always funny. It never changes...

Father Antonio's Black Label
By James Whyle

This is the story of a journey and of a grail that was found and emptied and filled again by magic. Every word of it is true. The journey was undertaken by the photographer and myself and liquor ran through it like water gurgling down a Madeiran mountainside.

Up in the dreamland of first class the photographer and I savoured Portuguese wines and Scottish malts. By the time we landed in Funchal, lack of sleep had added an edgy zest to the experience. The captain threw the engines dramatically into reverse. Fear dropped in like an olive. We stepped gingerly onto God's island.

It was clear from the start that Photographer and I were a recipe for an exciting new cocktail. Poured together into a small Avis car on the wrong side of a road consisting entirely of sharp bends and vertiginous overhangs, a road used by drivers of veiculo longos to practise for the Paris Dakar, we tended to arrive at our destinations both shaken and stirred: a Madeiran Martini.

Madeira is a gnomic garden that is always in blossom, a volcanic extravaganza rising lush and sheer from the green Atlantic. It is a place to make you understand that the Hispanic tradition of magical realism is no more than a mirror held to the world. It should come as no surprise that three hundred years ago the Virgin appeared on a hilltop to the villagers of Egreija.

Madeira is also an interesting place to switch to the other side of the road. The veiculo longos, keen to qualify for the rally, accelerate into the corners. And Madeira is all corners. Steep corners. There is really nothing you can do about the veiculo longos bar turning sharply into the gutter and stalling. The photographer was very helpful. I took charge of the centimetres between me and the speeding veiculo longos and he worried about the right-hand bumper. He veered between optimism and despair.

"You've got plenty of room," he would say. "Fine this

side." And then:

"Fuck!"

The photographer and I were really excited when we got the Avis car to Funchal. Even more so when we spotted our hotel, the Savoy. Then it disappeared. We'd see its enormous shuttered Spanish visage and try to approach from a different angle. At the last minute we'd be distracted by some small crisis, like a traffic circle, and Mr Berardo's hotel would vanish into thin air. Its elusiveness was as magical as father Antonio's bottle of Johnny Walker Black Label. The hotel was as ephemeral as its owner, Joe Berardo.

Joe Berardo left Madeira as a youth and travelled to South Africa to make money. He started off selling vegetables to the mines. He lives now, when he is in Funchal, at the very top of the town in the small and stately palace that lies at the centre of the Monte Palace Tropical Gardens which are owned and run by the Joe Berardo foundation.

Because, for a South African, Madeira is a mixture between extreme foreignness and astonishing familiarity, because it is an island on which the extraordinary will occur, Joe Berardo once bought a painting from my friend, the painter, Carl Becker. Carl's work contains certain surreal juxtapositions.

"Why you put the car on the pole?" asked Mr Berardo. Carl sweated. How would he explain his ironic view of Johannesburg mine dump and Southern African society to his potential patron?

"You don't know, do you," said Joe Berardo.

Carl sweated.

"It doesn't matter," said Joe Berardo. "Is interesting. I take it."

Mr Berardo's hotel is all old marble and chandeliers. Early on the morning of our arrival a small bandy uniformed man was polishing leather banisters. Our chambers unready, we were ushered to the Bellevue Buffet on the seventh floor. It is as big as a rugby field, owns a view of the wide Atlantic, and is inhabited by one hundred and thirty-seven couples, all aged sixty-five. Barring the smallest variation in pastel, they dress identically. The men carry floppy white hats for the sun. They all wear glasses. They speak seven languages between them and they come for the flowers.

We understood why that afternoon when we drove into the flower parade.

"You cannot go to the Savoy," said the astonished policeman, "there is a festa."

Car abandoned in a parking lot, we watched as Funchal's sons danced past wearing uncomfortable life-sized papier-mache dolphins on their heads. Funchal's mothers had painted their shoes blue to match the dolphins. The floats were all made of genuine flora and one was crowned by an island girl with golden stars jingling on her nipples. I absconded and walked down to swim in the Savoy's warmed seawater pool on the rocky shore. I was a lone character in a movie in Eastern Europe until one of Mr Berardo's men came and offered me a towel.

In the morning the photographer and I hit the roads and got lost. Within hours we had cemented our relationship by saving each other from certain death beneath the wheels of veiculo longos which approached at great speed from the unexpected direction. We turned north and drove over the central spine of the island and down to the coast at Sao Vicente. Sao Vicente is a hardware shop and a cafe and a couple of houses in a garden landscaped by Samuel Taylor Coleridge in an opium dream. Down on the shore water oozed from the rock where the buildings were cut into the hillside and majestic Atlantic rollers crashed on the shore. We drove through streaming rocky tunnels to Porto Moniz. Along the way precipitous steps led to vineyards that clung to the mountain. Often the road was just wide enough for the car and I offered sincere Catholic prayers to the saints at every bend.

And then, in the afternoon, we came to Egreija. We stopped at Egreija because Father Antonio put into the mind of the photographer the thought that he would like to buy a pair of boots. And so we looked at the boots in the shop and had a beer. Outside, Paulo the carpenter and the shop keeper's husband were putting up the wooden frames for the flowers for festa to celebrate the appearance of the Virgin on the hillside above the village three hundred years before. It became necessary to take photographs of them. Then the photographer became happy and charming and he directed other inhabitants of Egreija to sit in the light in the entrance of the shop so that he could photograph them also.

It was only in saying goodbye that we introduced ourselves and shook hands with Paulo the carpenter and tried to hide our astonishment at the feeling of the stumps of the fingers which he had lost many years before in an accident and about which he was philosophical. Paulo's name is Paulo Lorenco Caldiera and he worked for many years in Van der Byl Park near Johannesburg. He took us to see the church and his workshop and on the way we passed the house of Moses Acafrao, the mayor of Egreija, who for many years owned and ran the Outspan Cafe in Sundra in Johannesburg and the Sundra Cash Butchery. We got talking, the major and I, and before long I had to call the photographer and tell him that we had been invited to taste Mr Acafrao's wine which was pure and new.

The mayor explained that when the wine became old he took the thick residue from the bottom of the barrel and distilled from it an Aguadente much more powerful than the wine which owned only "eight or nine degrees of alcohol". It became necessary then to taste the Aguadente also and we liked it so much and were so lavish in our praise of the mayor's vegetable garden and his pigs and his chickens that the major gave us a bottle.

Then father Antonio arrived. Father Antonio speaks no English. He is eighty-eight years old and his pale eyes have faded to allow the light of God which shines strongly on the inside of his head to have access to the world. We were instructed that we would visit him in his house.

"Very clever," said Paulo of Father Antonio, "four passports!"

"But they don't hear," said the mayor, pointing to his ear, "we must look after them."

Father Antonio's eyes gleamed through his spectacles and he spoke happy and excited words of which we understood nothing but the good will from which they emanated.

"He is the biggest authority in the village," said the mayor, and then he paused for a long time, "on religion."

Father Antonio had a preliminary errand to attend to and so we drove down the hill in the Mayor's old right-hand drive South African Merc to see his vineyards. We parked on an eight hundred metre cliff. Far below, nestling next to the sea, were the vines whose produce we had tasted. The grapes, and sometimes the mayor, made the journey up and down the cliff in a small metal basket. On Madeira a mini cable car is the farmer's equivalent of a tractor. The thought of the journey was enough to give me gibbering nightmares. Fortunately Mr Acafrao could not demonstrate the mechanism as the cable had recently snapped.

Father Antonio's house is a fine square double storied building in the centre of Egreija. Its orange tiles and white walls and dark green shutters are sparkling clean. They are devotedly maintained, like the dark and gleaming interior, by the villagers of Egreija. In the dining room, Father Antonio sat on one side of the table and the photographer, the mayor and I sat on the other. Paulo the carpenter and the mayor's son remained outside. Father Antonio produced a bottle of Johnny Walker Black Label, four tumblers and a cake. Christ watched from the cross on the wall. Father Antonio broke the cake and poured generous measures. We raised our glasses. The whiskey tasted like ice cream. We spoke. The mayor translated. Father Antonio beamed at me, interrogated me. I told him my marital status. The mayor referred to him in the godly plural.

"They say: 'Married with three children - very rich people!'"

Father Antonio rose and produced two more cakes and another bottle. These we must take with us. He looked at me with merry eyes, indicating the cakes.

"For the wife and children!"

I guarded those cakes carefully on our travels and brought them home. For a time I carried the whiskey also but one night we got drunk on The Algarve and I borrowed some money from the photographer and the next morning I couldn't remember how much it was. The photographer said he also couldn't remember.

"Look," I said, "why don't you take the scotch and we'll call it quits."

And so it was. But when I arrived home my wife had offered refuge to a friend and the friend had left a present. There on the dining room table, gleaming by divine intervention among the fruit bowls, was the grail offered to us by Father Antonio, there, reincarnated, was Father Antonio's bottle of Johnny Walker Black Label.

Long Legs and Hot Music
By Lawrence Poole

Dedicated to the immortal Louis Armstrong

Imprecision. That's the word I'm looking for. I need to describe something that's not precise. Or, at least, something that's not *quite* precise. I'd love it to be precise, but it won't damn well *get* precise.

I have a piece of music to tell you about that, at this imprecise moment in time, I happen to think is the greatest piece of music ever laid down by any group of human beings anywhere. Ever. You'll disagree, most likely. But, to be precise, you can fuck off. You want to talk about your own taste of music, you write your own story.

If you open HD on page thirty-seven - I know, you don't own a copy. As it happens, neither do I. The copy I have here is Brigid's. If I hadn't met her in that bar, I would never have even heard of it, most likely. Isn't it funny how chance things like that, inexplicable attractions and imprecise motivations, can affect our lives so much? There I was, unhappily knocking back a drink. I can't remember what I was drinking. Memory can be so fucking imprecise, can't it? I was in that bar, and I'd have had a fucking dull day at work. I can be perfectly precise about that. And I saw Brigid.

She was with some other people. I was almost definitely on my own - it was just a quick-stop drink for me, a swift visit to the watering hole before I went on with my journey. Nothing to celebrate, no special occasion. Just another interruption before the inevitability of whatever was going to happen next in my life. Getting the metro home, most likely. I suppose something may have been in store for me on the way to the station, like tripping up on a paving stone, or perhaps looking in a shop window and seeing my reflection. Who knows?

Anyway, that's where I met Brigid. In that bar. She was talking to some people. A small group - mainly men, mainly Indians. The precise details of those people, of that bar, escape me now. But I remember Brigid. That first time I saw her. She's pretty tall, Brigid. About five eleven in the old money. Ha, fuck. *The old money.* We seem to have gotten through a few currencies since I first heard anyone say *that*. What currency are we using now, even? I've lost track. I think it's all done with plastic now, isn't it? Some computer juggles a few figures about, and works out how many rupees to remove from the running total of my life that's known as my bank balance.

Anyway, there's Brigid. She's wearing jeans. Her legs are something, I can tell you. I guess you could call me a 'leg-man'. Hattie, my girlfriend, has damn fine legs, also. The way a woman stands on her legs, fucking does it for me every time. I fucking know - *what else would they stand on?* Wiseacre. They'd look a bit fucking foolish crawling about on the floor or balancing on their hands. The fucking way, I said. The fucking way they do it. Posture, I mean. Poise. Style. Balance. And that line of the spine - how the line of the leg is continued in the small of the back, and up through the shoulders, the neck, the balance of the head, the tilt of the chin, and back down the front; the shape of the breasts seen through the clothes, the outline of the bra, the slight tantalising impression of nipples, the roundness of the belly, the fuck-me-if-you-dare swagger of the hips, the bend of the knee, the imprecise way the angle of the heel sets up the sexiness of the ankle as it toys with the notion of impossibility, somehow still standing, at odds with comfort. And that face, arched eyebrows, almost cartoon-like really, plucked in that style that seems to suggest constant curiosity, surprise, sexual allure and frankly a dash of plain, vain stupidity on top. Her lips, thin and lipsticked, that sort of lipstick that you just know is going to be a nightmare for the barman to clean off her glass. Her hair: obviously dyed light blonde, obviously originally light blonde. What's the fucking point in that? I'm a man, don't fucking ask me. It's cut tidily, stopping just above her shoulders. Not flashy, but it looks good. *She* looks good. Her ears may be a bit big, come to think of it, but that's being super-critical. So what precisely makes my cock warm when I look at her? I think it's that smile. When she smiles, the lines on her face, the lines that have built up on that face after almost forty years of framing that smile, appear all around her mouth, across the cheeks, form an arc coming down from each side of that long, slim nose. Those eyebrows manage to go up even higher, pushing her forehead into corrugated folds against her pulled-back hairline. Her eyes, green, like, well, fucking green. I don't know enough about greens to give you a precise green. Listen, her eyes shine. They fucking shine.

And so, there I am in that bar with my drink, feeling pretty fucking imprecise. And my eyes are looking round the place, seeing what shreds of interest they can pick up in the short time it's going to take me to drink my drink, and I see a small group of people. Mainly men, mainly Indians. And they're not tall. I know some Indians are as tall as the next man, but these are the shorter versions. I don't know about that stuff, different strains, gene-pools, castes. You tell me. Actually, don't bother. I don't care.

So, there's this group of mainly short people. Mainly men. Mainly Indians. And I'm looking imprecisely at their backs, and my gaze moves up over the dark, gelled hair, worn in some strange sticking-up style that I suppose is meant to make them look not so short, or male, or Indian. Whatever. And above and beyond these heads, these fucking green eyes shine at me out of that face, full of lines created by its smile, and I feel some imprecise connection. Something I can't describe. Those fucking green eyes. If I didn't know better, I'd say they looked straight into my fucking soul. Brigid once told me she felt precisely the same way when I first introduced her to Hattie.

Anyway, this piece of music. I've got to tell you about it. What's it got to do with precisely anything? I don't know. I'll tell you what, though. It's got everything to do with me. You can skip it if you like, if you're busy. Skip the whole rest of the story, if you want. It won't bother me none. Skip away - I'll lend you a fucking rope if you like. You can go read one of those proper stories. You know, the ones that have a beginning, a middle, an end. And you empathise with the characters. Fuck, go read that shit. Go find a story about someone who reminds you of yourself, or someone you might have been, if you weren't fucking *you*. Yep, this is the bit you'll want to skip. Just like a scratched record. Which, by dint of a fucking neat piece of authorial coincidence, is pretty much what it's about.

I'd beaten Hat home, by hours. Of course I had. I'd fucking skived off work not much after midday. I had managed to get from Nangloi station to our apartment without much incident, and was doing my hands-in-pockets, focussing-on-nothing shit when I got in the door. Almost walked straight into the door, most likely.

Maybe I was thinking about Brigid's legs, I don't know, but I needed a drink. I soon fucking dealt with that need. But I needed a fix of something more than booze. I had to open HD and get my nose into some serious fucking personnel lists. Although they probably call them fucking *human resources rosters* these days. Cunts.

I sat in my armchair. In my right hand I had the gadget. It did everything, that fucking gadget. Turned the music on, adjusted the central heating. Amazing the stuff they come up with to make our lives less complicated.

Anyway, I'd got the gadget pointed at the sound system. On the table in front of me was a fucking large tumbler of whisky. Don't you love the way tumblers are named after the effect they're going to have on you? Next to the whisky,

I had the best fucking intoxicant I know: Brigid's tattered old copy of HD.

It's a book, in case there's any confusion. I know some of you probably don't remember books. 'The New Hot Discography; the standard directory of recorded jazz.' That's what it said on the cover. It also said: 'compiled by Charles Delauney. Critirion. 1948.' If you're bothered about details. I'm not that bothered about details, myself. The fuckers slow me down too much.

Obviously the book had lived a long life and come a long way, to be keeping me company in my living room in Delhi that afternoon. What was the reason for my fascination with it? Fuck knows. I'd need to know how my mind works to be able to tell you that. Part of it was probably the fact that it wasn't mine. If I had my own copy of the fucking book, I'd most likely have lost interest in no time. Sometimes I'd do my best to practically hijack that book, I needed it so much. When Brigid went for a piss or something, I'd hide it accidentally under a cushion, or put it absent-mindedly in a drawer, hoping she'd forget she'd brought it with her. Got away with it sometimes. And that's how I came to be sitting that afternoon, with a huge glassful of whisky, HD open on page thirty-seven, and the gadget poised in my hand. I'd hidden the book under my armchair while Brigid and Hattie had been talking in the kitchen the night before.

What was so great about page fucking thirty-seven? It had this information on it:

'TIGHT LIKE THIS'
Louis Armstrong and His Savoy Ballroom Five
Chicago 1928
Louis Armstrong - t-v-speech
Fred Robinson - tb
Don Redman - cl-as-speech

Jimmy Strong - cl-ts
Earl Hines - p-speech
Mancy Cara - bj
Zutty Singleton - d

You think that looks boring? Fuck off, you thick cunt. What do you know about anything? And you should have skipped off to read *The Lord of the Rings* anyway.

So, I hit the PLAY button on the gadget, and for the next three minutes I forgot about Hattie, work, and Brigid's legs. I'd disconnected all but one speaker of the surround-sound system, and out of that sole speaker came a crackling noise sounding like fat spitting out of a fat fuck of a sausage. That's what they used to sound like, records. You probably don't remember them, either, do you? I love that sound, it's like a come-on. Gets me horny as hell, especially when its followed by a quick trumpet intro that gives way to a little honky-tonk piano. I could tell you that the piano was played by Earl Hines. In Chicago, in fact. In 1928. And all the rest. But I don't fucking need to, because if you look up a few lines you'll find the blessed Monsieur Delaunay has furnished with you with that information on the very wonderful page thirty-seven of his very fucking wonderful book. And I have been equally munificent in passing the information on to you. That's the kind of nice guy I am.

What he doesn't tell you is that over said piano there are two voices talking utter crap. One sounds like a woman. No, that's not true, it sounds like a stoned black man trying to sound like a woman. Or a stoned black man trying to sound like a stoned black man trying to sound like a woman. I don't know. Fuck what am I, a music writer now? Anyway, this hokum female voice says,

'Oh, it's tight like this.'

To which a male voice, presumably Satchmo himself, responds:

"No. It ain't tight like that either."
"I say it is tight like this."
"Let it be tight like that then."

I know, it's total shit, but all great art needs flaws. Just like drunks need them to keep them going. So, 'Tight Like This' starts with this baloney, and I'd heard it a hundred times before, so I leaned over to HD and tried to count how many fuckers there were in the fucking Savoy Ballroom Five. While I was wondering about Armstrong's math, the music was busily swinging away, working up its alchemy, wrapping itself around me like a benign spell. Have you *really* never heard it? Fuck, it circles you like a cat, looking for a place to dig its claws it.

A clarinet wafts in and out, the piano runs up and down a few scales. I'm listening to it now, as I write. The trumpet and a trombone nonchalantly pick out a figure, almost pretending they're not there. They, in turn, concede the floor to an unassuming piano solo. God, even now, knowing what's coming next, I'm lost for fucking words. Anyway, let's get back to Delhi before I end up describing the damn tune twice.

I closed the book, and leaned back, cradling it in my arms. Fuck, I loved that book. So *fucking* much. How sad is that? Brigid always said I was a sad sack fuckwit. I guess I always knew she was right, deep down. Anyway, the piano solo ended, and I've closed my eyes again. I'd close them now but I can't write with my eyes closed. And Louis's come in with two notes that there really are no words for, apart from to say it was like he was heralding something unspeakably ominous.

There's a pulsing rhythm starting up, like the band are marching and standing still at the same time. That's what it seems like anyway. Sorry if I'm all over the place with tenses and all that stuff here. It's a bit fucking hard listening to the same piece of music at different times simultaneously. It's a bit like marching and standing still at the same time, in point of fucking fact.

The pulsing riff kept on doing its thing, and Louis' trumpet is moaning away over the rhythm like he's a kid who's rocking backwards and forwards in sadness but with no tears left to cry. You know, like when you're so fucking sad no amount of booze is going to help. And I'm holding onto HD, with my eyes closed, rocking back and forth too, as the rhythmic tension keeps on building around me, and I'm thinking I've got nothing left; the trumpet's crying quietly, like it's feeling the same way, and the hokum girl's voice joins in saying,

"Ah, it's tight like that, Louis,"

as if there's been an argument going on and a point has been conceded.

But the trumpet hasn't conceded nothing, and it continues to swirl around the melody like someone racking their brain for the right words. Fuck, those right words are so hard to find. Another male voice chips in with,

"Oh it's tight like that,"

but still the trumpet mused, like it was rubbing its chin one last time, looking for those elusive words. And then it finds them.

I held tight to HD as that trumpet soared. It fucking filled my senses, illuminated the cunting air with its sadness. Tears fell from my eyes and I could taste their salt on my lips, as that trumpet wailed defiantly in the face of every indignity it had suffered or would ever suffer. That was one fucking defiant trumpet Louis played. He didn't need words, he had his own fearful wordless poetry that you won't find in any fucking dictionary.

When Louis was all done crying, the second male voice said,

"Ah, it's close like that,"

and with another crackle it was over. I shivered and took

a long slow drink of that whisky.

'Tight Like This' did that to me; took me away. HD, too. Those lists of recording dates and record labels, to Hattie they were lists of names and numbers, but to me they were a code, a key to a world where culture matters more than cunts, where art is more important than assholes.

Later that evening, me, Hat and Brigid were listening to some shitty pop song while we were eating dinner.

"Can you put the normal sound back on, Frank?" said Brigid. "I like this one."

I reconnected all the speakers, and soon the sound was pounding from the walls and floor.

"That's better."

I looked at a crack in the ceiling, hoping I might find some solace there. I found precisely none.

A G-bag A Day

By J A Hudspith

Advertisement
WARNING - CONTAINS SEX, SWEARING, SPIDERS AND SMOKING. LOOK AWAY, SHOULD ANY OF THESE THINGS TURN YOU OFF. CERTIFIED U by G-bag Corp.

One urban myth would have us believe that the admen at Coca Cola turned Santa's coat from green to red. Born from such a myth, the G-bag is now legend itself, yet its success brought a multitude more myths to muse - many mocking and scorning the glorious product. The corporation realised that such disdain has become typical of everyday life, often showing little regard for others and the future. Therefore, before the G-bag goes the way of Santa's coat, G-bag corp. has decided to nail its origins right here in hard copy. The G-bag is no myth - it is legend - let it remain so!

***

We join the Rind family just before they hit the big time. They could have lived next door to you, or on that dodgy estate over the way. You know the one.

School's out for Summer, and Rolland Rind, seventeen, is on the bus home, studying his art assignment with hungry eyes.

'URBAN MYTHS AND LEGENDS - PROVE, DISPROVE, DISCUSS'

This is right up his street. He's sitting next to his brother. Ray is three years younger but just as excited, grinning and hissing and pointing at the list. It was certainly up his street, too, and with Rolland's video camera in mind, the ideas gushed.

"What about this one?" says Rolland.

1) STARS CAN BE SEEN IN DAYTIME IF VIEWED FROM DOWN A WELL

"There's no fucking wells round here," Ray says.

Rolland nods agreement. "Yeah, pile o'shite anyway. Look, here's the `pissing in a pool` one."

"I'll do that'un," Ray says, grinning.

Rolland shakes his head. "Nah - can't take a camera to the baths these days. Too many paedos knocking about."

Ray shrugs and continues following Rolland's finger.

"This one," Rolland says, "`Get rid of warts by selling them` - you've got warts - "

"Two," says Ray, holding up his left thumb.

"Well that's a start. And there's this one - `Tap a pop can on its base to prevent foaming` - that'll be easy enough."

"Yeah but boring," Ray says. "Find something better."

"Here's one - `Smoking - Inhaling through the filter end will result in erectile dysfunction` - you're always playing with your cock. Up for it?"

Ray laughed and squeezed his crotch. "I'm game."

"Our stop," Rolland says as the bus lurches, indicating the descent to the Melaney estate.

Mum and Dad weren't due in until six, so Rolland and Ray settled in the heat of the garden with a few of Dad's beers and the video camera. It was a second-hand Sony and not the best. Dad had got it cheap, online. The battery only lasted two hours tops and the cracked casing was held together with electrician's tape, but it still worked and had a cool feature for switching to night vision. Rolland's favourite. He'd used it to prove that Ray played with himself in his sleep. Rolland reminded his brother of that and pointed to another on the list.

13) MEN THINK ABOUT SEX EVERY SEVEN SECONDS

"Dunno about men," Ray laughs. "I think about sex every second. I have an image in my head - all the fucking time - of that chick, what's-her-face, her with spiky hair and zits."

"Vicki?"

"Yeah. She showed me her fanny behind the co-op last Christmas eve. Cost me a fiver and it was minging. Hairy as fuck. And thing was, she'd come on and didn't know it. Horrible it was. Like an ape with its face ripped off."

Rolland howls, and Ray joins him. Bottles clinked, the sun shone.

Deciding the `tapping the can` one might be fun after all, Ray brought six cans of Coke from the fridge and Rolland filmed as he tapped the base of each on the wall and got thoroughly soaked by the subsequent spurting.

"That was a good'un," Ray says, wiping his face in his tee shirt. "What's next, bro?"

The sound of buggy wheels comes up the path. It's sister Riana pushing baby Mary. She miscarried twice before succeeding with Mary, but now sixteen, she's turning out a good mother. Mum says that Mary is a godsend.

"Sis," Rolland nods. Riana smiles and trundles past.

"Agoo," Mary says, throwing her dummy out.

"We could do this one," Rolland whispers.

Ray comes over and reads. "*Mixing dog food with baby formula will cause baby to explode within a week.*` Great - we've got a baby!"

"I'm kidding. Sis'd fucking kill you, you knob. Be serious. I think we should do the inhaling one. You said you were game."

Ray necks the rest of his beer, throws the bottle on the grass and says, "Go for it - I'll go nick a pack of Dad's fags."

Dad had built the shed years ago. Now it was close to falling down. Ray positioned himself behind a work bench and Rolland sat on the lawnmower, with the camera ready.

"You're not filming my dick," Ray says, dropping his pants.

"Got to," Rolland replies. "No proof otherwise." He chucks Ray an old rag. "Hang this on it when you're ready."

So Ray grins and whacks away behind the bench with a packet of Dad's Bensons opened and ready.

"Okay," he says, and steps out from behind the bench with his pants round his ankles and the rag pointing skyward. He takes a cigarette from the pack. "Quit looking," he says.

Rolland laughs and Ray jumps up and down on the view screen.

Ray lights the filter end, sucks hard, then spits. "Eurgh, tastes like shit."

"Keep going," Rolland says. "Another three fags at least. And squeeze your plums or something or you'll go soft."

Ray turns his back, does a little shuffle, turns back restored. He lights another Benson at the filter end.

"Suck hard," Rolland says.

"I fucking am," Ray says spluttering, then lights a third and sucks and sucks but still the rag points skyward.

"Can't feel no difference," says Ray.

"Stay still while I get a close up," Rolland says, so Ray stands hands on hips like Superman and shouts "Da-dada!" with the rag balancing on his cock.

"Okay, put it away." Rolland snaps the camera shut. "Let's buy your warts!" So they write out a contract affirming the exchange of 10p and the fact that Ray's warts now belonged to Rolland. But nothing happened to the warts.

"That's another in the can," Rolland says. "What next?" He scans the list and finds one. It seems to shimmer on the page. He somehow knows it is the one.

23) WE ALL SWALLOW EIGHT SPIDERS A YEAR WHILE ASLEEP

Ray argues they wouldn't have time to conduct such an experiment. Wouldn't they need a full year?

"Not if we up the spider count," Rolland says, knowing deep down that this one was going to be a winner. He didn't know how. He just knew.

The shelves in the shed were dusty and cobwebbed. "There'll be plenty spiders in here if we look hard enough." And so they set to work.

Mum's Cellgo slimming pills came in handy at this point. Forty or fifty old tubs filled the shelves. They contained screws, nails and whatever else dads put in tubs. They emptied one each and began hunting for spiders. Rolland used an ice scraper and captured two. Ray used his hands and caught a whole lot more.

"Fuck me," Rolland says, keeping his distance from the prickly mass of black in Ray's tub.

"Got about forty, I think," Ray said proudly. "And an earwig!"

***

So Rolland fixes the camera between the legs of a large Victorian doll on a shelf on Mum's dresser. He tapes over the ON light and does a few test shots, marking the best position in the dust between the doll's feet. He sets the timer to kick in at 1 am and drapes dolly's lace hem around the camera. It was all set.

By midnight, Dad was snoring. By half-past, Mum was muttering in her sleep. At ten to one, Rolland gives the nod.

"Where'll I put them?" Ray whispers, rattling the tub of spiders.

"On the bed, dickhead."

Ray gets down on his hands and knees and creeps along the landing in the darkness, Cellgo tub tucked under his chin.

The bedroom door is closed. He grips the handle, turning

it slowly until it clicks. Dad's snoring continues. He opens the door an inch and peers in when next door, baby Mary cries out in her sleep. Only once, but it's enough to make Ray sweat. He waits. Nobody stirs.

Still on hands and knees, he opens the door just enough, crawls through and slowly unscrews the top off the Cellgo tub. Heart pounding, he reaches up and shakes the tub over the duvet, retreats quickly and closes the door carefully behind him. He hurries back to his room where Rolland waits, eyes glaring.

"Done," Ray whispers.

Rolland laughs and dives under the covers.

***

Mum and Dad had already gone to work, and the second Riana leaves for an appointment with social, Rolland and Ray retrieve the camera from between the doll's legs and check the bedroom for spiders. They find none at all which seems odd, so they go to their room and plug the camera into the TV.

The camera position had been perfect. Dad's head's on the right of the screen, snoring, mouth hanging. Mum on the left, neck craned. The first hour passes slowly. Mum mutters something occasionally. Dad lifts his head and opens his eyes at one point. He stares straight at the camera. The night vision made his eyes green and weird.

"Not a single spider," Rolland says. "Where'd they all go?"

"Look," says Ray. "I see one!"

He was right. It was on the headboard and moving towards Dad. Rolland rubs his hands together and Ray moves closer. They stare as the spider - one of the larger, hairy things Ray had caught - leaps from the headboard and lands on Dad's pillow. It crawls over to his open mouth, steps up onto his bottom lip and slithers inside.

They both gasp and Ray shouts `Holy fucking shit!` and jumps around the room. Rolland grabs him and pushes him to his knees in front of the TV.

"Shut up and watch, eejit!" He slaps the back of Ray's head and gets down beside him just as the next spider crawls across the pillow.

"Jesus fucking Christ," Rolland mutters. "What the fuck have we done?"

Ray is shaking his head.

This spider is smaller and faster. It runs across the pillow, skirts around Dad's mouth, scuttles over his neck, jumps to Mum's ear, and disappears inside.

"Fucking hell," they both say at once.

More spiders run a trail down the headboard. The trail splits into two and they're crawling over Mum's and Dad's faces, vanishing mostly into mouths. One big black hairy thing pushes its front legs up one of Dad's nostrils and squeezes inside. When it vanishes he snorts and splutters. At the height of the action, spiders queue to get in mouths - medium sized ones push into nostrils and small ones burrow into ears. Mum smacks her lips occasionally which makes Ray want to puke.

They run the film back and count spiders. Okay it's night vision, it isn't easy to pick out individuals and the count could have gone a dozen either way, but this was way above anything Ray had shaken on the duvet.

"Sixty? Seventy?" Rolland says.

"Yeah," Ray nods. "About that."

Discussions go on all day. First they checked Mum and Dad's room. No spiders, so Rolland sent Ray up to the loft. Poking his head through the trapdoor was as far he'd go. There were no spiders. Well, the odd web in the corner, but nothing unusual.

"We need to do it again," Rolland says. "With baby

Mary."

So they set the camera up in a clothes basket, aim it into Mary's cot directly where her head would lie, borrow one of her smiley face nightlights and stock up with a case of Red Bull.

"No way am I sleeping ever again," Rolland says.

"Damn right," Ray agrees.

So they sit up all night facing each other, perched on the edges of their beds with their trousers tucked in their socks and their feet up on books, lit only by the smiley face nightlight and they watch the wall behind each other for arachnids.

Dad snores and Mum smacks her lips now and then making Ray shudder every time. Baby Mary doesn't stir.

Next morning when the front door closes and they're alone once again, Rolland and Ray pelt up the stairs.

The picture crackles and Mary is on screen. Three little spiders are on the baby's cheek. One by one they slip into her mouth. Mary shoves her thumb in after them and sucks. And that was all.

"Only three?" Ray says. "I don't get it."

"Three's bad enough," says Rolland. "Don't you see? Nobody can sleep ever again!"

"No shit!" Ray looks confused.

Rolland sends him for more Red Bull so he can be alone to think.

"Coincidence," he says on Ray's return.

"Huh?"

"The spiders we - *you* - set free in Mum and Dad's room attracted all the others. The fact that by the following night there were only three in Mary's room goes some way to proving that."

"Maybe babies just don't eat so many," Ray points out.

"No, I'm right, I know I am. We'll set up again tonight in Mum's room, and if I'm right, then there'll be no spiders at all."

"S'pose, " Ray shrugs and opens a Red Bull.

Neither of them eat today. They watch Mum and Dad at the tea table as if they might be aliens about to flick out their tongues and zap flies.

"You two on speed again?" Dad says. "Red eyes and no appetite. You can't fool me. Lay off it!"

And that was that until bedtime and the smiley light gets plugged in and Rolland and Ray perch on their beds, watching the walls. But Dad isn't snoring. There's a tapping on the wall. It's the headboard.

"Fuck - they're shagging," says Ray and both shove fingers in their ears and stare at each other for what seems an eternity.

Morning eventually comes, the house is theirs once more and the camera is retrieved.

Bleary eyed, and hesitant to watch his parents screwing, Rolland plugs the camera to the TV, the screen crackles and the film begins.

Ray crosses himself, jokingly. "Can't believe we're doing this," he says. "If we get copped with this, we're fucked."

Rolland shushes him. They stare at the screen as Mum makes the first move.

"Why's she tickling him?" Ray whispers. "Fuck me, his dick's tiny!"

"Shush," Rolland says. "And quit fucking whispering."

Ray shuts up and they watch as their mother straddles their father and he wriggles on his back and bucks and the flab on her sides wobbles.

Ray makes gagging sounds and Rolland slaps the back of his head.

"Look," Ray says, as Mum, still straddling Dad, begins to knee up the bed and rub herself on his chest.

"This is so wrong."

Rolland agrees. He was glad the camera showed Mum

from the back.

She puts her hands to the wall above the headboard and gets up on her knees. Dad slides down below and Mum grinds on his face.

"Holy shit," Ray whimpers, pulling a face. "Vicki's fanny is banished from my mind forever."

"Jesus, Jesus," Rolland mutters repeatedly while Ray makes the gagging sounds again. But then it's over. Dad's soon snoring and Mum's smacking her lips again.

"Here they come," says Ray as a spider appears on the headboard. Then another and another, trailing towards Mum's mouth, jumping through smacking lips one after the other.

"There's none going to Dad," Ray says.

"It's his face, look at it," says Rolland. A circular patch of luminous green covers his mouth and nose.

"It must be off Mum," Ray says. "Where she rubbed in his face."

"No fucking way!" Rolland says.

"You know what this means," Ray says, excitedly.

Rolland looks at his brother.

"We can sleep. All we need's someone to sit on our faces and I know just the girl!"

Vicki arrives promptly.

"Two's up is fifty quid." She peels off her sweater and unclips her bra.

"Erm - all we want is you to sit on our faces for a bit," Rolland says.

Vicki chews on her gum, and eyes him up and down for a second. She shrugs and kicks her denim skirt off. "Thirty then," she says, letting her knickers fall to the floor.

Ray moves behind, pointing at Vicki's muff with a hand clasped to his face. He was right. The fucker was hairy.

She catches Ray laughing so does him first, writhing on his face. Rolland notices the lump in his jeans and the wet patch forming. Dirty fucker.

He lies on his bed waiting his turn impatiently, knowing that sleep would come soon and the spiders would wait for another day. When Vicki climbs on, Ray is already snoring. When she climbs off, Rolland's eyes are almost closed. He grins with the sweet taste of Vicki on his lips and falls to deepest sleep.

"What the fuck?" Dad's saying, which brings them both round. He's watching the film of his little pointy dick and his wife on his face and that's when he finds his new product and the G-bag face pack is born. Buy yours today, only 4.99 for thirty applications. Never sleep again without a G-bag on your face. Wear it and save humanity. A G-bag a day, keeps the terrors away!

THIS WAS AN ADVERTISEMENT FROM G-BAG CORP

The Peter Chair

By Jasper Dorgan

The dream offers no respite, even in the scald of the daylight hours. It mugs me in the blackness, or in my chair, or under the stinging roar of my grey-time shower. As with all things in this world my dream comes unbidden, but it is master of my realm. It is the dream.

It comes and lays me down on my back in a deep hole and I am wedged between the solid sides of an open pine box that is slowly, relentlessly compressing me with the indifferent power of a car crusher. I am unable to move. My shoulders and my legs are clutched, my head is locked in a stone-pillowed vice and my bones are enwrapped.

I am stiff with fear.

I look up at distant stars, thick-framed by the dribbling black walls of a pit too high to touch, and too deep to fathom. My skull is cold, all air is distant. I scream at the top of my voice.

"I ain't dead yet you bastards!" But no-one hears because no sound can escape. Then the first spray of earth falls from out of the stars and peppers my arching crotch with hot fists of fury. Another fall blankets my feet and my shoes are filled with pebbled soil and worms. I twist and turn and burn against the box sides and man-age to release a raw and numbed hand a few inches above my tomb's slow buckling rim. Soil rains in on me and the stars are drowning. I stretch out the chewed bone of my hand and heave the television on.

Mrs. Ritka and Mrs. Brewer are the breakfast girls. That's what they call themselves. They are both fifty if they are a decade. All people lie.

"What would you like for breakfast?" asks Mrs Brewer. She is as round as a cricket ball. Her movements are constant and sure and her clawed and mottled hands never stop doing.

"I would like scrambled eggs, kippers and fresh orange

juice, please."

"How about some porridge? Porridge is your favourite."

"My Shannon's Tyrone has insisted on crushed blue velvet," says Mrs. Ritka. She takes a corner of my gown and wisps it over my head as if un-sanding a beach towel on a sea blown breeze. She is small and sturdy and has never once looked me in the eye. But she sponges me in talk every morning. "He hasn't thought of the poor bridesmaids. Young Kayla is not shaped for blue. Especially crushed."

"Velvet is a magnet to spills. Church settled?"

"Would either of you ladies care to give me a blow job?"

"He's got Frankie Foyle's mates as ushers. In cream tails. I mean its asking for trouble."

"I'll let you keep your teeth in,"

"That's men," said Mrs Brewer. "All creams and crushed blue,"

They jerk and lever and press and shuck me into my clothes. This is how the wakeful time begins. My sunrise. I roll and flop and burn as sheets are peeled from around and under me and my clothes are wrestled to me. Then I am planted in my chair. Mrs. Ritka and Mrs. Brewer do their work with remarkable efficiency. They crease and flip me into my world as if folding sheets on laundry day. On my good days I can imagine Mrs Ritka and Mrs Brewer to be the St. Trinian's Upper Fifth hockey team gang-raping me. Good days are when I succeed and when the breakfast girls get me dressed, nozzled, re-bagged and pointed at the television in under rape recovery time.

Mrs Brewer always puckers into the door mirror and applies new lipstick on her departure.

"We're gone then."

"Go fuck!"

Through my day window I can see the town roof-tops that flow like rubbled lava down to the river that I cannot see for the obstructions of grey buildings and greyer trees. The townscape will make me move my wheels when cars crash or when violent weather attacks, but it is a dull view for the most and not worth much battery.

Except for the house on the hill. The house on the hill is always interesting. I never have to waste my wheels to see the house on the hill. It is framed in my window. A small castle on a hilltop that is skirted with trees. I know its every stone and brick, its every window and tile. It is a fascinating house. It is the home of the leaping man. I see him often. The man with the wild red hair. He never walks through the candle-lit rooms of the house on the hill, he only leaps them.

Television is my one friend. I can shove it on and off and over. Tell me something sadder.

It is a really good day when Tasha visits. She sometimes comes with her mother in the early evenings. But never often enough. Mrs. Prakova does my tea and tidy and tucking in if her Dimitri isn't home from the trucks. She does her work well and happily. She even talks to me. She is one of my finer warders.

Tasha came with her one day. Mrs Prakova introduced her daughter to me and asked if I minded if she waited. The college bus had been missed. I am a gentleman, how could I refuse?

> I love my jokes. I really make myself
> laugh sometimes.
> I must laugh.
> I am the funniest person I know.

Tasha sat on the end of my bed chewing a large cud of gum on a slow rinse cycle. She stared at me. People either stare or look. The look is always elsewhere. But Tasha is a starer. Her mother is scrubbing the shower in the next room. Tasha's young face is apple-bloomed from the recent pant of missed buses. Her blond, dark-rooted hair is warrior spiked, her eyes panda rimmed. She sits on the edge of the bed with giraffe legs stretched out from a pleated skirt and her zip-top straining on a burgeoning swell. Hail to thee, St. Trinian.

"Can he see and hear like?" Tasha had shouted.

"Oh yes, I expect so," Mrs. Prakova was somewhere on her knees in the bathroom. "Just he probably don't understand it much. Poor boy. Be nice."

"How old is he?"

"Twenty-six I think. It is on the form."

"No way! Kidding yeah? Ten years older than me?" Tasha looks me up and down. It is not a long journey.

"What crap he is wearing? Not exactly a style Jack is he? Does he understand us?"

"Ah, that only God knows I think."

"I would love to see you naked."

"Can't he move anything?"

"Three fingers on one hand. A little bit. He can switch on the television."

"I hope that your breasts are young like rugby balls and that, down below, your grasses are dark and damp and unmown," Tasha looked at me. Her turquoise lips stilled on the cud.

"Has he always been like this? Just sitting in a chair?"

"Yes, all his life."

Tasha leaned towards me. She smelt of strawberries. She spoke quietly.

"You poor fucker,"

She blu-tacked her gum to the headboard and stood up before me. She glanced quickly towards the bathroom and then slowly unzipped her top. Nut-nippled breasts tumbled out into my world. Tasha stepped back and then thumbed her panties to her knees and lifted her pleated skirt. She braced herself tall and let me feast for gone moments. Then she was dressed again and sitting on the bed as her mother came into the room wrestling with buckets.

Tasha heard me. She gave me voice. And hope. And I don't know whether it is a precious gift, or a torture, to long so for missed buses.

There is a bar in the basement of the house on the hill. It is lit in amber glows and I can hear music weaving faintly through the night. Some nights there is singing. And flinging. I imagine being drunk must be like a half wipe-out. The moment of rippling warmth when the world melts at all its edges and you just don't give a fuck anymore. Just before the drips black in. I would like to try beer. I haven't had brown. And maybe even to vomit. Tubed grey just doesn't do it.

I can say cunt anytime I like. To anyone. But I don't much. I think it a lot but I don't say it. It is a discipline I give myself and I am strict. I have the freedom to say whatever I like, whenever I like. But every freedom has a price. Mine is a deaf world. So I talk to myself and I am good company. Known myself for years. We can say anything to each other. Like. Men know in their marrow that they are all rapists and all women know themselves sluts. I only speak as I know. And I always tell myself the truth. Like. I know that everyone checks their shit in the bowl and that everybody in the whole fucking world is a cunt. See. Anytime I like.

The Peter Chair

When Mrs. Brewer washes and combs my hair I know I am to go visit with the Governor. I am wheeled along the corridor of closed doors and into the lift and down across to the polished wooden meeting room that always smells of work. The Governors are doubtless kindly thinking men, but they are still cunts. That will be my last until green. I promise me. I must not let my-self down. Discipline and dignity.

> Everything is ironic. Trust me.
> I always will.
> I have to.

Dr. Andrews wears bright red shoes and has a grey pony tail that nestles between his shoulders. He is the latest Governor. My fourth. He wears jeans and a rainbow woollen jumper and he dreams of rock bands.

He smiles and half-rises as I am wheeled in squeaking across the floor. Seated at a far table a couple of not-heres in public authority jackets are finding interest in my files, which this season are a pastel blue. Dr. Andrews ushers a chair aside with his foot to facilitate my parking and to show me that the feet in his red shoes are working.

"Hello Peter, how nice to see you. You are looking well to-day."

"I am not Peter,"

"Now you know the drill. Just a few simple questions. Now you say as you find, eh? No holding back!"

"My name is not fucking Peter. I am not Peter! I never have been Peter. I have been telling you for ten years." A woman wearing a green button-over and big-bowed, snow white trainers connects the answer lead to my chair stick. People are mostly shoes.

"Now just yes or no. As before. You remember Peter?"

"I am not Peter. Peter escaped. Your predecessors fucked

up the paperwork when we all got zoo-trucked here. It was chaos. You branded us monkeys all wrong. The computers went fuck. I got Peter's file. But I am not Peter. Peter escaped, the bastard. He's been gone for eleven years."

"Yes or no, OK Peter? Now, tell us, are you comfortable here?"

I have become Peter. Even though I am not him. I have never met him but I am him. Or I have been for too long to really believe. I do not quite remember who I was before I became Peter. Too much orange fluid has passed over my tongue. So I am Peter. It is only the naming of chairs.

In my clearer periods of still I often see Peter tramping across fields and hiking woods and singing with a swinging cane along the cobbled streets of a Disney town. I wish him dead. I answer yes and no correctly to all Dr. Andrew's questions. It is the quickest way to leave. My answers only ever change the colours of files

The dream comes again. Hush.

My television is obsessed with clothes and food and football. My only friend is a bastard. Friends are like that. But television has told me about sex. It is a gentle and harsh teacher. I saw kissing young. I think it must be like a very quick battery re-charge. Kissing always makes people energetic or lit.

In my child time, television showed me the holding of hands and the cuddling, often with singing. For many years I thought babies were made from bike rides into the countryside. I don't know why.

But Marlon showed me the fucking. He is a quiet nigger in blue overalls and puke yellow baseball boots. He has two stances. One is hanging on his mop like a condemned man chained to a dungeon wall, the other is with his boots up on

The Peter Chair

my bed watching television with me. We watch television all through the darkness. Marlon brings popcorn.

"What you watching this shit for? Want some popcorn? Oh yeah. Tough kid. How about some fluid? Gotta have juice for the telly, man. Any football?"

Marlon takes the console and channel flicks.

"This all the shit you got on this mother? Can't you get no cable?"

He went to the back of the television and did things to it. The television revealed what it had hidden from me all this time. Naked, panting women of every colour, creed and contortion strobed across the screen before me. Blond ones and redheads. Raven and bald. They bowed and kneeled and spread before me. A banquet of sex.

"Titties on that one too ballooned. That aint' no real tittie. Don't go for them gals, boy. Like slubbering on a beach ball. Woa! Is that chick albino?"

Through Marlon I have come to know and see the things of sex. Of its function and variety. Its crazy positions. I think sex must be an ecstatic pain. Though for whom and why it is difficult to tell. But I do know that black men are better at it than anybody else. Marlon told me. He shares his knowledge with me in the darkness times. I know that all women have vaginas and it's not just the younger ones. I had imagined they healed over with age. The knowledge that even Mrs. Brewer still had one set me quiet through several greys.

But it did not matter because I was not going to have any sex. I am not built for such wrestling. I haven't even done holding hands.

Then Marlon flicked to a new sight.

"Oh get on down there, my lady! Pump that bitch!" I came to from a small melt to see a woman under red silk hair slowly eating a branched prick right down to its collar. She and the collar were having a good time. So was

I. There was a sex for me after all. That I could do. Or have be done.

Yeah, like fuck.

> Stay calm. You know what happens
> if you get angry.
> It's not like you've had it to miss it.
> And nothing can change.

I don't watch sex too much anymore. I watch programmes about giant cats bounding with arched backs and liquid speed across savannah grasslands and bringing down gazelles. It is my porn.

Mothers always tell their daughters lies, so Mrs.Prakova lied to Tasha. It is true that I can move three fingers of my hand, but I can also move my head a little. And my prick also moves. Mostly by itself and at a colour of it's choosing. Mostly grey. My prick is an idle pet mushroom living in my cellar. It grows as it pleases and dribbles as it needs. Most of the day it just lays there, a small fungal cluster sucking a humid dark. But the prick-drip changes often seem to interest it. Or a hot shower maybe. Sunrise without fail. Then it becomes a stumpy and rigid twig. On good days, when Tasha visits, it can bloom to host a sail.

Mrs. Brewer and Mrs Ritka ignore my morning twigs. They share a mixed glance of stretched night-gown and thin-pursed lips and then flip me face down onto the bed and go away to find some-thing else to ignore. I lie arse-up, jacked and spiked on the bed, my face being sucked by the plastic sheet, until my twig either buckles or snaps. And as much as I scream at it the twig never chooses to sag. It always snaps. It is painful. Every morning I bargain with the mushroom not to twig. But my prick is as deaf and as defiant as the world. My prick really couldn't give a fuck for me.

> I really am the funniest person I know.
> I have to laugh. Have to.

Mrs Brewer only returns when I am snapped and flattened.
"Now can we get on?" she asks the sheets.
"Is a hand job too much to ask?"

The house on the hill has a high, round brick tower with stepped windows carved into it like a tree-house ladder. A flag often flies from the tower-top pole. Every day the walker comes up through the trap door in the top of the tower and takes his walk around the turret with his binoculars hung to his chest. He wears a cap and walks his sky-high path slowly with his body leaned forward as if against a stiff breeze and his hands knotted loosely at his back. He walks with a slow and contemplative tread. He stops every few paces and pulls his binoculars up and gazes at the distant view. He compasses his tower, stopping and watching through binoculars at every segment of the visible sphere.

I never wonder what it is to walk. I can no more imagine the ground's press as I can the sun's burn. But I often wonder what everywhere looks like.

> The dream has come. Hide still.
> It passes quicker that way.

I have lived twenty-seven years and I still suckle at my mother's breast. She cradles me and wraps me in her arms. She slaps me across the bottom when I am being childish or morose. My mother has grown strong in my care. She can turn on a star. Her engine under my seat is as big as a box and her pockets are swollen with bottles and masks and pills and pastel blue papers tied in green ribbon. Behind every great man there is a chair.

> I have pissed myself.
> I really am so funny.
> And we'll be lying in your
> funniness all night.
> Or fuck dreaming on a water bed.
> Stop it.
> Too late.

It is a little after orange. Not too long until green. I can tell by the smell of chemical sweetness drifting in from the landing. And Baywatch is on the television. Orange is the middle feed. It smells of caramelised sugar and tastes of nothing. Nothing ever does. It's just orange. It is grey soon after the sunrise and green when the sun goes low. My life measures in colours.

Bobby takes me out sometimes. He is a large, round man with a beard and he wears outdoor boots and oil stained jeans. He wraps me up in blankets and wheels me through the park of mud and swingless swings and along the canal path to the pub. He parks me under the smoker's roof at the back and I watch laundry drying on the back yard line while he takes beer inside. Then he wheels me back to my room.

"Looks like you could do with a massage," he says. He always does.

And he undresses me and flips me face down on the bed and kneads my back. I do not feel it. Nor do I feel him entering me. I am only aware of it because of the short sensation of bouncing that dizzies my head and my panted breath mists the sucking plastic about me. It never lasts long.

It is of no matter. It is no more than the clunk of wheels on un-even pavement slabs. A bargain for the price of a laundry line. Bobby will then clamp me over the bath and scrub my arse with a loofah and Johnson's All Surface Cleanser Cream. I drip wet from my arse all night. But I don't feel that either. Only the mushroom does.

The house on the hill has a room in the cellars. It is a bright lit room of soft-cushioned armchairs. And it has no mirrors. Or blank television screens. Or polished chrome. A room without reflection.

I rest there often.

On the first year of my death some people made themselves a cake and tied a balloon on mother. They blew out twenty-one candles and clapped because I had not yet died.

My television tells me that there is bad weather forecast with a possibility of local flooding. I like bad weather. It means the buses might not be running.

On the very top floor of the house on the hill there is a room with a large double bed and a lockable door. A log fire burns in the grate and the mirror is turned to the wall. Tasha sits on the edge of the bed, smiling as someone unzips her top. I see that it is Peter.

> I sense its faint rush,
> like autumn leaves rustling
> on a bow-wave of breeze.
> It comes again
> on the hooves of horses.
> To lay me down once more

Jasper Dorgan

And the pit seems deeper
The box tighter
And the stars more distant still.

Bliss: A Love Story

By Patricia J. DeLois

The Kings Hill kids partied at a cottage on one of the lakes. Not Moosehead, but one of the smaller, more exclusive lakes. This place belonged to Shaun's roommate, Peter, or to Peter's parents, although no one could remember ever seeing them there. They had other homes, I suppose, in trendier places, and it seems they didn't consider it worth the trip to Maine to visit either the lake or Peter.

They called it a cottage, but it was a house, right on the water, with thick woods all around. For privacy, they said, but in the winter, when I was there, it seemed eerily isolated, a good setting for a horror story. The frozen lake, the bare trees, the animal tracks in the snow. In the right light—twilight, for example—it looked menacing.

I was seventeen when Shaun first brought me there. Peter greeted us at the door.

Most girls thought Peter was better looking than Shaun—bigger, more muscular, perpetually tanned—but he knew he was good looking, and he was arrogant.

"Congratulations, Felicia, you're our first townie. We usually just fuck them in town and leave them there, but Shaun seems to think you're something special."

"Ignore him," Shaun said. "He's jealous."

I stayed close to Shaun as he introduced me around. Mostly people I'd met before, but one girl named Crystal was new to me. Heavily made up, with eyeliner that matched her dress—seafoam green, puffed up with petticoats, bows and ribbons everywhere. Her hair looked stiff, bleached ghostly white.

"Have you found your bliss?" she asked me.

"My bliss?"

"Find your bliss, or you'll never have peace."

"Tell Felicia about it," Shaun urged her. "I'll be back."

She talked for twenty minutes about her bliss. As she talked, she leaned to one side and then the other, moving her arms in fluid arcs, bending her wrists gracefully, dancing, like a demented ballerina in a looted jewelry box.

She found her bliss when she had her daughter, and she wanted to have another, and another, and fill the earth with children.

"In fact..." she glanced around, leaning in confidentially. I glanced around, too. Peter was watching us. "...I'm going to get pregnant tonight."

"Really?"

She smiled. "You might, too."

"Not me," I protested, but she shushed me as Peter approached us.

"Peter's experiencing turbulence," she announced. "He hasn't found his bliss."

"Mine was never missing," he said. He cupped his hand over his crotch and leered at me. "I got plenty of bliss right here. Want to see it?"

"No, thanks."

"Maybe later," he said, and then Shaun came back with some dope. We all got high, and I forgot to mention to him that his friends were creeping me out.

*

I'd waited a long time for this date with Shaun, ever since we'd first met.

I was fifteen, at a party in the woods behind the high school. Separated from my friends, I wandered among clusters of drunken teenagers, some from town, some from Kings Hill—there wasn't much mingling. I came upon a group of private school kids blocking the path, and instead of moving aside to let me by, they widened their circle to include me. Somebody passed me a joint. It seemed only polite to stay for a while.

A boy with blond hair was telling a story. I don't remember the details, only that he told it with a dry, self-deprecating humor. The story had to do with his parents' willingness to spend large sums of money on anything that would keep him away from home. I thought it was courageous of him to offer up the sad fact of his unwantedness for his friends' amusement.

As he finished his story, he caught sight of me, and it occurred to me that it might be one thing to joke with his friends about a situation they were aware of, and another thing to expose it to me, a stranger.

"I like you," I said.

He didn't hear me, but he read my lips, or my eyes, and he smiled. Someone else was bitching about his own parents, with less humor and more bitterness. Shaun and I continued to smile at each other until a red-haired girl in a leather jacket appeared at his side and slid her arms around his waist. She turned her face up to be kissed, and I had to walk away.

At subsequent parties we circled around each other, progressed to chatting whenever possible, but it always ended the same way, with one of us saying regretfully, "I'm here with someone." For two years this went on—I had almost given the whole thing up as hopeless, and my friends said it was just as well, because boys from Kings Hill were never serious about girls from town—and then one night we were both without dates, and we talked to no one but each other all night, and since then we'd been together, making out and dry humping every chance we got.

Despite their concerns about the boys from Kings Hill, my girlfriends were thrilled when Shaun invited me to the cottage. Take notes and make a full report, they said. Were the Kings Hill parties as wild as everyone said they were?

Shaun warned me that although the road was plowed—a service Peter charged to his parents—it was steep and treacherous. No one would be driving home after dark.

"Can you spend the night?" he asked.

It was a big step. I told my parents I had an overnight baby-sitting job, and got permission to be out for the night.

*

So I was at the party, taking notes, and while they were an eccentric and colorful crowd, with a flair for drama, so far I hadn't seen anything wilder than our own parties. I learned that Crystal's baby was a year old, living with her parents, being raised by the same nanny who raised Crystal.

"At least she still has a job," she said.

I felt like a guest of Gatsby's, surrounded by rich, careless people. They had all been in trouble. Most of them had been to rehab at least once; they all had psychiatrists. They appeared to be living adult lives; in addition to therapy, they talked about lawyers and trust funds, and custody arrangements.

I lived in a Catholic town where people didn't get divorced. I had never heard such litanies of step-families, half-siblings and part-time parents. No wonder these kids were fucked up.

I will say this: they were generous with their drugs. Everybody there offered me speed, mushrooms, cocaine. I settled for pot laced with hash, and I had a nice buzz. I was excited about spending the night, sleeping with Shaun. I was falling in love with him, and I was happy.

I settled in the living room, which seemed spacious even with three long sofas arranged in a horseshoe around the stone fireplace, a picture-perfect fire blazing. Not one, but two black bearskin rugs on the floor; someone had arranged them into a sixty-nine.

Shaun was sitting on a sofa, and I was perched on the arm, my feet in his lap. We were talking to the guy next to him, about skunks, of all things, nocturnal creatures, when the girl sitting on the other side of the guy whispered something to him, and then she was on her knees, sucking his cock. Just like that. Within moments there was another guy behind her, with one hand up her skirt and the other undoing his belt.

"Shaun?"

"It's okay, they're just partying." He stroked my leg.

"They're having sex," I whispered. For some reason I thought my observation might embarrass them.

"I know," he whispered back. "I probably should have told you."

Probably, but it was too late now; I was too distracted to discuss it. I didn't mean to stare—how rude—but I couldn't believe it, not only the threesome but the whole party continuing around them as if nothing were happening. I suddenly felt far too stoned—unable to move or speak.

I watched as the girl reached for Shaun. Her hand groped for his leg, then moved up his thigh, pausing briefly on my foot, up toward his crotch. He caught her hand and moved it away; he murmured something in her ear. The cock in her mouth muffled her response.

He sat back, looking pleased with himself. He smiled at me. I don't know if I smiled back or not.

And now everyone was getting into this new phase of the party. On the opposite couch, Crystal was on her elbows and knees, preparing to be impregnated. A couple on top of the bearskins, another on the floor behind me. Over on the third sofa two naked girls were making out, and beside them, also naked, sat Peter, leaning back against the cushions, stroking his erection and surveying the room with an imperial air, as if deciding where to put it first. His eyes rested on me. He smirked.

This shook me out of my stupor, and I got up and stumbled into the kitchen, where people were still acting normal, thank God.

Shaun followed me.

"I can't do that," I said.

"I don't want you to. But I was hoping you'd want to get it on. With me."

"Jesus, Shaun, you could have just asked."

"Do you want to?"

"Just with you," I said.

He took my hand, and led me upstairs to the master bedroom suite. He locked us in.

"Just you and me," he said.

So while everyone else was downstairs fucking, Shaun and I were making love for the first time.

I'd been with boys before, but nothing as sweet as this, nothing this slow and burning. He held me close, kissing my lips, my throat, my shoulders, my ears, my hair. We were moving together, closer, deeper, breathless. At one point I almost cried, aching with tenderness as he took my nipple in his mouth.

After a prolonged and delectable entanglement, we found the rhythm to carry us through, and afterward, when we lay still, he said, "I don't know about you, but I think I just found my bliss."

*

The bedroom had a wall of glass and a deck overlooking the lake, which glowed with pinkish-orange light as the snow and ice reflected the dawn. Colored light sparkled through the frost on the window, casting an appropriately rosy luminescence throughout the room.

We hadn't slept—I'd lost count of the number of times we made love—but we had enough energy for one more romp, and then we showered together, and said, why not, what's once more? By the time we made it downstairs we had fucked ourselves stupid, and could only laugh and giggle as we tripped over the bodies of his friends, who lay where they fell, or fell where they lay after last night's escapades.

Only Peter was up, making coffee in the kitchen.

"You missed a good party," he said.

"I don't think so." Shaun opened the stainless steel refrigerator and pulled out a bag of oranges. "I don't think we missed a thing."

"Well, people missed you," Peter said. He was leaning back against the counter, his arms crossed over his chest. Something about the way he said "people" suggested a specific person, someone who would remain nameless in my presence. Another girl who wanted Shaun for herself.

Shaun shrugged. "There are plenty of other people to play with."

He tossed me an orange, and I sat at the table and peeled it. He stood beside Peter at the counter, dropping his own orange rind into the sink.

Peter shot me a contemptuous look. "What about her? Is she going to play?"

"I don't know, let's ask her." He gave his peeled orange to Peter and started another one. "How about it, Felicia? Do you want to play?"

"Just with you."

"Just with you," Peter mocked me.

"Hey, come on." There was only the mildest reproach in Shaun's tone. "You don't have to be such a prick."

"Yes, I do," Peter said. He was sulking. His coffee was ready, and he poured himself a cup.

Shaun volunteered to chop kindling. He put on his coat and went out, leaving me alone with Peter.

"I had a really good time at your party," I said, remembering my manners. "Thanks for inviting me."

"I didn't invite you."

"What's your problem?" I asked.

He looked at me steadily—I think he was trying to stare me down. "I think he could do better."

"Maybe. Maybe he doesn't want to."

"Apparently not. But you won't last. I know him, he'll get bored with you."

"Then what are you worried about?"

He ignored the question. "We're roommates, you know."

"I know."

"We're very close. Like brothers. We share everything."

I nodded. "That's great."

"Closer than brothers."

I nodded again.

"You don't know what I'm saying, do you?" he said.

"That you're close?"

"Go home," he said. "Go back to your little townie friends. You have no idea what you're getting yourself into."

By now the others were waking up, hung over, wandering into the kitchen in search of coffee and juice. Shaun came in with a load of wood and got the fire going again, and I never thought to ask what it was I was getting myself into.

*

There were more parties, every weekend, and Shaun and I attended, up to a point, after which we withdrew to be alone. My failure to participate in the full range of activities caused resentment—not so much my refusal to share myself, although there were some complaints about that, but more, I think, my refusal to share Shaun. He belonged to them, and they were used to having their way with him, and they saw me as selfish, even though Shaun told them it was his own choice not to play with them any more.

We stopped going to their parties. Shaun would get a

room in town for the weekend, and sometimes we went out with my friends, but mostly we stayed in his room making love.

"Did you like having sex with all those people?" I asked him.

"It's fun if you're wasted. Otherwise it's a lot of work."

"Is this a lot of work?"

"This is easy."

But it wasn't. His friends were giving him a hard time; they required him to take a stand against bourgeois monogamy.

As his friends turned away from him, he clung to me; I was the remedy for his loneliness even as I was the cause of it. He was different from other boys I'd been with, who were willing to share the pleasures of sex, but for whom there was nothing more to it. For Shaun, sex was an emotional experience, an outlet. When he was inside me, I felt his love, but I also felt his need. I felt the neglect of his parents and the rejection of his friends, and what he poured into me was the contents of his heart—his love, but also his anger and his sadness.

If Peter had known the extent to which his rebuke fueled Shaun's passion for me, he might have backed off.

*

The Kings Hill School had a different schedule from ours, and they were having a vacation the week of Valentine's Day. Shaun's friends were going en masse to Jamaica to practice their depravity in a sunnier climate; rumor had it that Peter wasn't going with them.

"He's going somewhere else," Shaun said, "or so they tell me. He's not speaking to me any more."

"Not at all?"

"Not a word. He acts like I don't exist. Anyway, he'll be

gone, and I have a key to the cottage. Valentine's Day, just you and me."

"Perfect," I said. "Just you and me."

*

He brought roses, and wine, and a box of chocolates. He cooked dinner, roasted chicken with mashed potatoes and gravy.

After dinner he built a fire and turned the lights out, and we ate some of the chocolates, throwing the ones we didn't like into the fire, where they melted into bubbly lumps that we said we would clean up tomorrow. We made love on one of the bearskins, naked in front of the fire, rolling around on fur that smelled of all the sex that had been had on it. When we were finished, we moved over to the other bearskin.

"We can't have anyone feeling left out," Shaun said.

Eventually we made our way upstairs to the master bedroom, where we lay in bed and listened to the groaning ice on the lake, and the creaking of branches. There was no moon; when you live in town you forget how dark the night can be. I felt like we were very small, just the two of us surrounded by a wilderness that was cold and harsh and a darkness heavy enough to crush us, but I wasn't scared, because we were together.

*

I had been sound asleep when the lights came on. For a second I was confused about where I was, and then I saw Peter standing in the doorway, snow melting in his hair and on the shoulders of his jacket.

"My God, this is romantic," he said. "Look at you two fucking lovebirds."

"Jesus, Peter, what are you doing here?" Shaun was sitting up, squinting in the light.

"I came to celebrate your perfect love." He stumbled into the room, drunk, maybe, or high on something.

He sat at the foot of the bed, facing us.

"This is great," he said. "Isn't this great, all of us together like this?"

I clutched the blankets around me. "What do you want?"

"Felicia," he said, not in answer to the question but more as a belated greeting, as if he hadn't expected to find me here. He smiled at me, and I was afraid. He had tracked us down for a reason, and it wasn't to celebrate our love.

He stood up. For some reason I remembered hearing that a black bear will stand on its hind legs just before it attacks. What I couldn't remember was whether you should stay still, or run.

Shaun slid out of bed. His eyes darted around the room, maybe looking for his clothes, but all of our clothes were downstairs. He pulled the comforter off the bed to cover himself. I slipped out the other side and took a blanket. He moved toward the window.

"Peter," he said, "let's talk about this."

"No more talk." Peter took a step toward him, and then charged him and tackled him. I might have screamed, but I couldn't hear anything over crashing of the plate glass as they fell through it and landed on the deck. They fought, but Peter was bigger and stronger. I wanted to stop them, but before I could reach the deck Peter was hoisting Shaun's limp body up to the railing and tipping him over the side. I heard a dull thud as Shaun landed in the snow. Peter bundled up the comforter and dropped it down after him.

"Don't freeze your nuts off," he said cheerfully.

And then he turned to me.

Too late, I ran for the door. I clutched at the doorframe

as he dragged me back into the room, but I only managed to hit the light switch, plunging everything into disorienting darkness again. The blanket was torn away from me, and he picked me up and threw me. For a second the darkness held me up, suspended in mid-air. I bounced hard on the bed. Before I could catch my breath he was straddling me, beating me with his fists. I fought back, but my blows were ineffectual, until I clawed at him and connected with his face, and then he hit me so hard I blacked out.

But not for long. Not nearly long enough.

I heard his zipper.

"Just you and me, Felicia."

"No."

He put his arm across my throat and leaned into it, choking me, while he worked one and then both of his knees between mine. I didn't know if he was crazy enough to kill me, but it seemed he might be; it seemed he was. I saw the police showing up at my house to tell my parents I'd been murdered at the cottage.

"There must be some mistake," Mom would say. "Felicia's babysitting."

They would be baffled for the rest of their lives.

He was between my legs, his arm pressing into my throat. He reached down and shoved himself into me, found my wrists and pinned them to the bed, and before I could even start breathing again, he was fucking me.

I couldn't get my feet between us to push him off, couldn't get the leverage I needed. I wanted to get him off me before he came; for some reason I was thinking that it wouldn't be so bad if I could at least stop him before he came, but my efforts had no effect.

"Yeah, you like that."

I denied it, but he paid no attention. I protested. I begged.

"I always thought you had nice tits," he said. I almost

puked as he took my nipple into his mouth. I couldn't see him in the dark, but the wetness and the smell of him made me want to retch. I started to cry.

"Don't be a baby," he said. "You came here to get fucked, didn't you?"

It occurred to me that just because he wasn't choking me any more didn't mean he wasn't going to kill me. He had all the time in the world, and nothing to stop him.

I called Shaun's name. I listened for him to break a window, or break down a door, I expected any moment to hear him on the stairs. I couldn't let him find me like this.

I quit struggling. I took a deep breath and opened my legs and moved with him, to hurry him up, because it didn't matter any more if he came, it didn't matter if he was going to kill me. I just wanted it to be over.

He moved faster, and he began to talk to himself, murmuring something I couldn't make out. The same thing over and over, like a chant, or a prayer.

"Please," I said, and he pounded into me harder. He bit my shoulder as he came.

For a minute he was motionless, and I held my breath. He lifted his head and chuckled in my ear.

"You see that, Felicia? You're nothing special."

"Get off me."

He didn't move.

"This has been fun," he said, "but I've got to go. I'm going to get up, but if you move, I will kill you. Do you understand that?"

"Yes."

He squeezed one hand around my throat; his breath was harsh in my ear. "I will break you in half, I will rip your fucking throat out with my teeth. Don't. Move."

He got up and struck me one more time with his backhand. He zipped himself up and staggered toward the door. He found the light switch; the brightness hurt my eyes, along with everything else that hurt. He was standing in the doorway facing me.

"I'm going to bring Shaun in and put him in front of the fire," he said. "Warm him up a little, and then I'm taking him home."

"You should take him to the hospital."

"I'll take him wherever I want, you fucking bitch, and if you touch him again I'll kill you."

I heard him go down the stairs, then lost track of him until a light came on under the deck. He was talking to Shaun, but I didn't hear Shaun answer. I was listening for his voice when I passed out.

*

And it was Shaun's voice that I woke up to.

"I'm sorry," he said. "I'm so sorry, I'm so sorry."

Peter was gone—Shaun had persuaded him to leave, but there was no guarantee he wouldn't return. Shaun carried the ax from the woodpile just in case. He helped me get dressed, apologizing the whole time, taking inventory of my injuries. He wanted to take me to the hospital, but I refused. He talked about going to the police; I was even more adamant.

"Okay," he said. "Okay, we'll get a room."

He checked us into the Holiday Inn.

For two days I did nothing but take hot showers and cry. I lay in bed for hours with my head on his chest, listening to his heart. It was the only thing that comforted me.

I finally called my parents to tell them I was all right—they had figured out by now that I wasn't babysitting. They thought I had run away from home, and I guess I had, but as soon as I heard my mother's voice, I wanted my life back the way it used to be.

"Stay where you are," she said. "We'll come and get

you."

"You're going home?" Shaun said.

"I have to. We can't stay here forever."

"No, we don't have to stay here. We can go away. I can get a job, we'll get married."

"He'll come after us."

"No, he won't. He won't find us."

"How do you know?"

"He'll move on," he said. "He'll find somebody else."

"You don't know that."

"It doesn't matter. I'll protect you."

I opened my mouth but didn't say anything. I didn't have to; he blushed .

"We'll go far away," he said. "We can go anywhere, wherever you want, Felicia, where do you want to go?"

"I want to go home."

"Please," he said. "Don't do this to me."

I left him there. I covered my bruises with makeup, and I went home with my parents and followed their rules. I stopped going to parties, stopped going out altogether. I stayed in my room and did my homework; I had no desire to do anything else. I was afraid to go to sleep at night. I cried all the time.

My friends thought it romantic, all those tears. They were under the impression that Shaun and I had been honeymooning, shacked up at the Holiday Inn, and I said nothing to contradict them. I didn't tell them what happened. Nobody knew but Shaun, and we would not be speaking of it. My parents had forbidden all contact between us.

But he wrote to me. I wasn't supposed to know that; my parents intercepted the letters, but after a few months my mother's curiosity got the best of her and she asked what he kept apologizing for.

"Did that boy get you in trouble?"

She thought I'd run off to have an abortion. Would that be preferable to the truth? I didn't know, so I said nothing.

I pictured Shaun in his room at a new school—maybe he got lucky this time and got a single—covering page after page with his left-handed scrawl, pouring out his heart, and for what? Letters I never received, apologies that made no difference.

It was too painful to think about him, so I trained myself not to. I started going to parties again. I drank; I smoked dope. I slept with other guys, but I didn't get serious about them, and I discouraged those who were serious about me.

I graduated from high school, went to the University, where I began an affair with my freshman psychology professor. He was the only person I ever told about the cottage. He offered me therapy in the form of role-playing rape scenes, which actually helped, but in return I felt obliged to play other games with him, the ones his wife refused to play. It ended badly.

School seemed pointless; everything seemed pointless. I left the University, drifted through a series of low-paying service jobs, and ended up working at a daycare center.

I feel sorry for children. They can't look out for themselves; they have no choice but to trust whoever is in charge of them. Better it should be me than someone who will do them harm, because you know there are people out there who will hurt them, and some kids have found that out by the time they're three or four. You can tell.

I was in my second year on the job when I had one of Crystal's children in my class, her fifth—she was married now, and still blissfully producing children—and it was Crystal who told me that Shaun was dead.

We were standing in the snow on the playground. It was the end of the day, twilight, and there were just a few children left to play among the long shadows of the snowmen and forts and tunnels they'd constructed earlier. I thought of that first night at the cottage, the night we found our bliss.

Crystal kept talking.

"For a long time after he left Kings Hill he was into some heavy drugs," she said. "Somebody told me he did so much speed that his heart just stopped."

His heart.

Witness

By Gillian E Hamer

"Suicide?"

"Aye. Looks it. Poor sod."

"Jumper?"

"Aye. Helluva mess. This your first?"

"Yeah... Jesus."

I turn towards the voices. Two uniforms behind me. One short and heavy-set, thick moustache and glasses. The other tall and thin, ashen-faced and wide-eyed. Together they looked like Stan Laurel and Oliver Hardy in a police sketch.

"Call it in. Make sure the ambulance is on its way. Go get some fresh air, Shelton. You look like you're going to hurl."

Shelton disappeared, didn't need telling twice. Hardy stayed put, shielding his eyes against the glare of the sun.

He shook his head slowly. "So, then. What's your name, laddie?"

"Bridges. Carl Anthony," I reply.

"Let's see if there's any ID." Hardy pulled a pair of latex gloves from his pocket and opened the denim jacket.

Up close I can see the grey in this moustache and a brightness in his heavy eyes. I can see the pain there, and I know he's been this close to death before. Many times. It's a stench he carries with him, like a cumbersome cloak around his shoulders.

He stands and opens a small black wallet, unclips his radio and turns away. I can hear him muttering but the words are carried away. I feel useless, unneeded. Surely someone should be asking me questions, taking a statement. As I rise and brush concrete dust from my knees, Shelton returns, his face slightly less green.

"Ambulance on its way, Sarge. Got the crowds under control, too; bloody sick bastards some of 'em."

"You get used to it." Hardy shrugged and nodded towards the onlookers on the far side of the car park. "So, who found the body?"

"Me," I reply. "What do you need to know?"

"Yeah, couple of people, actually." Shelton flicked open his notebook. "Young guy called it in, but didn't stick around. And the old lady name of ... er ... Mrs Clarkson. Came out to the bins and screamed the place down. In a bit of a state, she is. I got WPC Slater to take her inside, make her a cuppa. Hope that's okay, Sarge?"

Hardy nodded. "Yeah. I think CID is on the way. Apparently it's the second jumper from this block of flats inside a month. They want to check it out, starting to look a bit suspicious. They can take a statement from her when she's calmed down a bit. Don't need the grief, do we?"

"No, Sarge."

I want to ask how long that will take, not keen on having to hang around for the CID. My shift starts at two pm, and if I'm late again I'll be walking, even if finding a corpse makes one hell of an original excuse. I'm the main witness. I can't believe I'm being ignored, like I'm just another sick bastard hanging around to see how much blood there is. This isn't easy. Doesn't anyone care? Jesus, the police really are crap. My old man never had faith in the law. I used to think that was just cos he'd done a stretch, but now I begin to wonder.

"Should I just wait, then?" I ask Shelton. Hardy has his back to me.

"Let's get you all back behind the tape, shall we?" he replies.

I shrug and wander across the road, hands buried deep in the pockets of my jeans. I can't get the image out of my head, a thick stream of crimson dripping off the kerb and pooling in the blocked drain cover; it carries blackened leaves and a used lottery scratchcard in its wake. I'd never seen real blood like that before, never knew there was so much of it. I feel bile rise, and swallow down the vomit, wincing at the bitterness in my mouth. Hardly the way to treat your prime witness, is it?

I listen to the chatter around me. A mixed group of teenagers, old women and young mothers. People without work, my mother would say. But then they make up most of the residents here on Blackthorn Estate. Most of the high-rises have long since been blown to smithereens, but there's still three left here on Blackthorn. And let's say the people who reside there don't do so by choice.

"Head smashed open like a watermelon."

"Drugs is my bet..."

"Anyone see him fly?"

"Looked like that young copper was gonna barf!"

"Anyone know his name?"

"Bridges," I reply. "Carl Anthony."

"Think he worked in the coffee shop on the high street, you know the posh one that opened recent. Nice lad, studying at Uni. too. Wonder what he was doing on Blackthorn?"

"Drugs. It's always drugs round here."

"You don't know that, Ma."

"Course I do. Gangs and pushers. Pimps and pros. Nothing ever changes on Blackthorn..."

I tune out. They know nothing. Small minded and short tempered, most of them knew nothing but this kind of life. It wasn't my job to educate them.

I could tell them about foreign cities and hot beaches that would make their brains explode. I could show them such beauty in art and architecture that they would be left speechless. I could describe landscapes and views that would be outside their comprehension. I could try to explain how it felt to be trapped, really trapped inside a life you don't want – and how much beauty and freedom there was out there just waiting to be discovered.

But it wasn't my job. I was just a witness, here to do my

bit. Then get the hell out of this shit-hole and get on with my life.

I wandered away from the fidgeting crowd, somehow feeling contaminated by their macabre interest. I hovered near Laurel and Hardy, waiting for my opportunity to speak. They stood in front of the prone corpse, as if trying to offer some modesty, some means of privacy from the eagle eyes of the onlookers.

"I never understand it. Suicide I mean," said Shelton.

Hardy shrugged. "Not for us to understand, lad."

"Yeah, but why, Sarge? Has to be other answers, surely?"

"Desperation. Fear. Guilt. Money. Sex. Even illness. Lots of reasons."

Shelton shook his head. "Not good enough reasons. Not for me. Not to do that..." He gestured over his shoulder.

"People do odd things when they're desperate, lad. I think something just gives inside their head; they stop thinking logically. I've seen it before, many times." Hardy drew in a deep breath and exhaled with a shudder. "Don't say you get used to it. Never. But it stops affecting you quite so bad. It's one of the worse things to this job. That and telling the rellies. No doubt CID will hand us that on a plate too."

Relatives. I hadn't thought about that. I'd been so caught up in the shock and revulsion. This was someone's son, brother, husband, father. Who knew who would be affected by such a small step forward into the unknown. The repercussions were going to go on and on, like a tiny stone in a large pond and the ripples it produced. I could imagine the reactions, the disbelief, and the tears. I could feel the pain. Palpable.

That was if anyone cared. I hope they did. I hoped someone loved Carl Anthony Bridges enough.

Suddenly I felt a desperate sadness.

"How much longer?" I called across to Hardy.

"Ambulance is here. And CID." He nodded as a distant wailing filled my ears.

"Good." I reply. "I've got to get to work."

Shelton smiled and looked relieved to finally be able to move away from the body. The blood soaked into the pavement now, it looked like oil from a broken-down vehicle. A few flies buzzed around in the midday heat, and I could smell the bin store nearby. Something maggot-infested, rotting flesh perhaps. I shuddered and pushed the image away. I didn't want to think about decomposition and realities of death.

I felt the same relief and stood to one side to let the ambulance pass, its luminous yellow a break in the grey gloom of the surrounding concrete.

I realised I'd never seen the inside of an ambulance before. I rocked and rolled as the vehicle sped through the streets. Not sure why the blue light and heavy foot on the accelerator were needed. Carl Anthony Bridges was beyond any medical intervention.

Time stood still, but passed so fast. I'd drowned in a sea of questions, answers, enquiries and arguments, and before I knew it somehow I'd been nominated to accompany the poor soul to the local A&E.

Just because I knew the guy's name. And had found the body, I suppose. Still, if I lost my job because of it, who was gonna take the responsibility?

Long corridors of white walls and bright lights. And then a sudden dimness. I could hear a woman crying somewhere, loud racking sobs as if her heart would break into a million pieces.

I remembered Hardy's words. Relatives.

I pitied the poor Doc who was breaking the bad news.

I stood from one foot to the other. The covered corpse

on its own now on a trolley in the centre of the room. Images of horror movies filled my head. What would I do if the corpse began to sit up? Do? I'd run like the wind, that's what I'd do.

I took a deep breath and blew on my hands. The room (the morgue?) was icy cold. Had they forgotten they'd left me down here? Some witness I'd turned out to be. How much longer? I wanted this to be over. I had a life to live.

The door creaked open. I jump and bite down on my lip. There was a priest I recognised, Father Edward Parry. Affectionately called Father Ted by the local youth group. I meet his eye and give a small smile, hoping he can see I'm here by force not choice, an innocent caught up in a terrible tragedy.

Father Ted leads the sobbing woman by the hand. Her face is covered by a curtain of long dark hair, but her shoulders shake as she stumbles forward. Her other arm is supported by an older woman, grey haired and straight backed. Her eyes fix on the white sheet as the Doctor leads the small group forward.

He lifts the edge and I look away. I've seen the bruised face and the bloodied skull before. I don't need to go through that again.

The sobbing woman falls to her knees. Father Ted makes the sign of the cross and his lips move in silent prayer.

The grey haired woman nods. Just once.

"Yes, that's my grandson. Carl Anthony Bridges."

The voice pierces my consciousness, my vision clears. My roles reverse in the time it take the sob to escape my lips.

Dear Lord! No ...

I know this woman; I feel her pain. I can take this no longer.

I move across the room, taking a wide berth around the covered corpse. I touch the shoulder of the broken woman, hoping she can feel me. Hoping she knows I can offer her reassurance.

"I'm sorry, Mum. I'm so sorry. I love you. Forgive me."

The room is silent.

I can hear my own pounding heart. I know she cannot.

She hic-cups, her tears stop for a second. She lays her hand over mine and looks upwards. Her eyes focus on the furthest corner of the room.

"I love you too, son. I forgive you. Go in peace."

She slides her other hand beneath the sheet. Grips the cold fingers and squeezes. Her lips flutter into the smallest of smiles, and then disappear as she bows her head again in prayer.

I smile as I kiss her cheek. I straighten and embrace my Gran.

I make the sign of the cross to Father Ted.

My job is done now.

The Lord is my witness.

Incompetent Crew

By Jo Reed

An extract from: *How to sail up Plymouth High Street*

I'd always loved the sea. On childhood holidays at the seaside I had been drawn to the harbours, to the sights and sounds of boats of all kinds; I loved the pleasure cruises across the bays that my father took me on. I'd never really experienced sailing boats though, and when I married it was quite clear that my husband did not share my enthusiasm. I had succeeded, one year, in persuading him to come with me to take a week long course in the Solent in the middle of February, from which we had both returned, cold, wet and exhausted, to a broken central heating boiler. He made me promise never to suggest such a ludicrous adventure again. Nevertheless, as I sat huddled in three sweaters and an overcoat, waiting for the engineer to return the miracle of hot water, I stared with a sense of exhilaration at the piece of card that I had just stuck in the back of the booklet I had been given by the skipper. It said 'Competent Crew'. I put the booklet carefully on a shelf, and forgot about it.

Many years later, my two sons grown and gone, one to Brisbane, Australia, the other to a nearby town to make his fortune as a songwriter, my husband and I split up. I was fifty, single and broke. It would be nice to travel, I thought, see the world. It was something I had always wanted to do. Amazingly, though, I had never travelled abroad on my own. I had always lacked the confidence, especially with strangers. Also, I reminded myself, I didn't have the cash. I was idly sorting out shelves filled with decades of junk, when something slipped out and onto the floor, so dust laden that I had to brush it off to make out what it was. I found myself staring at my old sailing log book, my enthusiasm rekindling as I leafed through the pages to the certificate on which the words were still just about visible: 'Competent Crew.'

Half an hour, a quick internet search and a few phone

calls later, the die was cast. In the two and a half years since that day, my life has been filled with the most extraordinary experiences, in the company of the most extraordinary people. I have experienced despair, terror, triumph and pure joy of the unique kind that can only occur among those thrown haphazardly together with a single purpose in mind – not to look ridiculous in front of an entire marina of expert onlookers. I'm still a long way from becoming an expert sailor, but I'm learning fast. The most important maritime regulation that I've managed to grasp so far is one that I don't think has yet been entered into the syllabus. When it is, it will read: 'When involved with yachting of any sort, never take oneself too seriously.'

Of course, on my first nervous and ill fated attempts to enter the world of sailing, no one thought to mention that particular rule, and, as a result, I almost fell at the first hurdle. As I pored over the listings of various sailing activities on the internet, I soon found that most were way out of my pocket. The pages were full of terms that I wasn't very familiar with, like 'charter' (which seemed expensive) and 'skippered charter' (which meant even less to me and was even more expensive). Finally, I came across a section entitled 'sail training', which seemed more hopeful, under which was listed 'competent crew' and 'day skipper'. Both were more within my budget, and my logic told me that having already done a competent crew course, I probably wouldn't be allowed to do it again. Therefore, I thought, my best bet would be to sign up for the week long Day Skipper course. The dusty certificate in my log book was by this time more than ten years old, and I had completely forgotten everything that had happened in the only week of my life that I had ever spent on a yacht. Never mind, I thought. I would simply explain when I got there that I actually only wanted to sail around for a bit to get the hang of it, and all would be well. Then, my eye was drawn to some smaller print underneath. It said: 'These prices are based on candidates sharing a cabin.' At once I started to panic. Weren't most sailors men? What if... My mind started to boggle. Then it occurred to me that if I was the only woman on board I might be asked to pay extra to avoid unwanted company. The course was going to take every last penny – I couldn't afford extras. However, to my relief, at the bottom of the page was written: 'Women only courses will run if there is sufficient demand. Please ring for details.' I heaved a sigh of relief, and rang for details.

Four weeks later, in the first week of April, I arrived at the clubhouse in Portsmouth, instructions in one hand, a soft holdall and sleeping bag in the other. My cleaned and dusted ancient log book was in the pocket of an old hiking jacket that I had bought years ago as a raincoat and never really worn. Consequently I was very aware that it looked almost brand new, and that everyone in the bar where I was waiting was probably sizing me up as a pretentious newbie. Already nearly nervous enough to make a run for it, I clutched my orange juice and stared fixedly at the door, hoping that the instructor wouldn't be too long.

In the event it was about half an hour before I saw a large woman in full sailing regalia, complete with yellow Wellington boots, stride confidently into the bar, her imperious gaze sweeping round the room until it finally rested on me. I smiled weakly, while huddling into my raincoat, feeling rather like a mouse that had just been noticed by a pretty ferocious cat. There was definitely the hint of a regimental sergeant major about her as she marched firmly up to me and stuck out a hand.

"So you're one of my Day Skippers?" It was more a statement of fact than a question. "Got your log book handy?" she asked, thrusting out the hand again.

I nodded, pulled it out of my pocket and reluctantly handed it over. She sniffed, and as she started to rifle through it purposefully I decided that the time had come to explain my intentions. I didn't get the chance though, as another woman came up to us.

"Ah, and I take it you're the other one," the skipper declared. Like me, the newcomer, who introduced herself as Kate, looked to be round about fifty. Unlike me, she was tall, fit and confident. Nevertheless I felt slightly encouraged. It didn't last long though, as the skipper's eyes had fallen on the pristine, polished log book that Kate had presented. There followed a short silence while the documents were examined.

"Ah – you did your 'Comp Crew' last year," the skipper commented to Kate, nodding wisely. "And have you done much sailing since?"

"Oh yes," Kate replied airily. "My gentleman friend has a yacht, on the Hamble. We go out most weekends. I'm hoping we can take a look at it while we're here. It's an 'Oyster 56', you know."

Kate sniffed proudly, and the skipper at once looked eager. I had no idea what an 'Oyster' was, apart from an unpleasant tasting type of shellfish, and was beginning to feel well and truly out of my depth. Then came the moment I dreaded, as my book was minutely examined, and the beady eye, now containing a look of contempt, was fixed on me.

"This certificate is ten years old," came the accusation. "Your sailing log doesn't seem to have much in it – did you forget to fill it in?"

"No," I admitted, feeling myself blush furiously. "I'm afraid I haven't done any sailing since."

"And you're here to take 'Day Skipper'?" The voice was almost a sneer by now.

"Well, actually…" I began, taking my chance, but once again I was interrupted, as two more women appeared in the doorway. Immediately, I was forgotten.

"And here are my 'Comp Crew' people," the skipper beamed, giving me a last contemptuous glance before greeting the newcomers. One, Sandy, was, I learned later, fifty-eight. She was recently divorced, and had a new boyfriend who loved sailing. She was doing the course so that they could go on yacht charters together, an aim that the skipper found impressive. The fourth member of our crew, Jenny, was an expert dinghy sailor who wanted to make the move to large yachts.

"Right," the skipper said briskly, once the introductions were complete. "I suggest we take our bags out to the boat, and then eat here at the yacht club tonight. We can all get to know each other, and be up bright and early in the morning for a safety briefing."

My heart sank again. I had seen the prices in the club restaurant. The course details had warned me that 'some meals ashore' were not included. I had been thinking more along the lines of the odd portions of fish and chips. I wasn't in the mood to object though, and after rapidly chucking our bags into the saloon of what appeared in the growing gloom to be a frighteningly large yacht, we all decamped to the restaurant and made our choices from the cordon bleu menu.

As it happened, my fellow crew women weren't half as bad as I had anticipated. Jenny worked in local government, and although she was obviously an experienced dinghy sailor, she had never been on a large boat before and was clearly as nervous as I was. The only differences between us were that a) she at least knew how to steer a boat, even if it was a small one, and b) the skipper, who still perched, unthawed, at the head of the table, wasn't under the impression that Jenny had signed up to do 'Day Skipper'. Kate was something important in a local hospital. After a long marriage she had found herself alone, and her new boyfriend, the owner of the 'Oyster' and a consultant in the same hospital, was keen on having a partner who could handle a boat. Sandy's potted history was constantly interrupted by text messages from her boyfriend, but between pauses we were able to glean the fact that she had been married and divorced twice to and from the same man, was trying to maintain a lifestyle to which she had become accustomed, and had the idea that finding a well heeled yachtie might do the trick. Thankfully the evening petered out long before anyone thought to ask me for my life story, and as soon as coffee and chocolate mints had been dispensed and consumed, we made our way to the vessel that was going to be our home for the next six days. I was allocated the saloon, we were given a demonstration in how to use a sea toilet, and less than half an hour later we were tucked in our sleeping bags, fast asleep.

Any hopes I might have had that things would look better in daylight were soon dispelled. The skipper's lecture began with an overview of the galley in general, and the fridge in particular.

"And this is my food," she announced, once we had been shown how to turn the gas on and off and light the cooker. We each peered into the fridge, following the direction of the pointing finger. Stacked carefully into one side was a selection of salads, fruit and cold meat. "This is yours, here," she continued, and we obediently took in the pile of pasties, eggs, streaky bacon and extra thick sliced bread. The same arrangement applied to the cupboards, and my crewmates and I glanced at each other nervously. There followed a safety briefing, and we were all fitted with life jackets and harnesses. The moment I was dreading was fast approaching. Very soon, we were going to be asked to do something nautical, and while I was sure my companions would have no qualms, I still hadn't managed to explain my position to our formidable skipper, and was beginning to feel terrified.

My fears, as it turned out, were entirely justified. My idea of taking the boat off a pontoon involved taking half the pontoon with me. In answer to a request to tie a bowline, I dutifully turned the cockpit into something closely resembling a half eaten plate of spaghetti. When asked to 'bear away' I turned the boat into the wind. 'Luffing up' almost resulted in an accidental gybe. By the time I had worked out the direction of the wind my turn on the helm was over. Even when I wasn't looking, I could feel the skipper's despairing shake of the head. My crew mates seemed to think the whole thing amusing. I, on the other hand, spent most of my time trying to think up ways of jumping ship without being seen.

By the end of the second day I still hadn't had an opportunity to catch the skipper alone to try to explain my situation. Things were made worse by the fact that she never seemed to eat with us. She never joined us as we sat round the table each morning for a hearty breakfast of bacon and eggs. Most lunches were taken on the move, and while we ate sandwiches and soup she would disappear down to the chart table. Evening meals were all taken ashore at local pubs – thankfully far more down to earth establishments than the yacht club – and then she would join us briefly, usually for a light salad, before excusing herself on the grounds that she had to check the tides/weather/charts etc. for the next day.

If the skipper's behaviour seemed a little unusual, Sandy's was downright odd. Each evening, as soon as the mooring lines had been secured, her first act was to leap off the boat and rush to inspect the shower block of whatever Marina we were in. She would then return, moments later, a look of supreme disappointment on her face. Jenny, Kate and I were at a loss. We had so far moored up at fairly well equipped marinas, and saw no reason for her obvious dissatisfaction. Sandy was clearly not about to offer an explanation, however, and none of us felt able to pluck up enough courage to ask. On the fourth day, however, the mystery was solved.

We arrived in Cowes just after lunch. Kate and Jenny had moored up and cast off from an empty pontoon several times, and I had succeeded in narrowly missing an expensive motor cruiser whilst elegantly nicking the bow on a concrete pylon. We finally settled ourselves in a berth not far from the pub, and my three crewmates went exploring while I stayed on board, hoping for an hour of peace and quiet to brush up on some knots. I was in the cockpit trying to work out why my clove hitch had transformed itself into a granny knot when a shadow looming over me announced the arrival back on board of the skipper. It was too late to hide the tangled length of rope in my lap, so I reluctantly met her disapproving gaze.

"About time we had a little chat, don't you think?" she remarked, brows beetling ferociously. "How would you say you're getting on?"

I didn't think that was really meant to be a question, but I'd had enough, so I answered it anyway. In a fit of pure frustration I blurted it all out – the whole story, together with an accusation that I would have spoken out a lot sooner if she hadn't been so stand offish in the first place. After all, I protested petulantly, a skipper who can't even eat with the crew doesn't exactly give off an aura of approachability. I came to the end of my tirade and folded my arms, out of breath and feeling deflated.

The skipper stared at me in surprise, and then a sheepish look came into her eye. She sat down next to me and took up one of my jumbled attempts at a recognisable knot. We both fiddled with ropes for a while, then she said glumly, "I'm on a diet. The trouble is, sailing makes me hungry, and every week I get groups of people on board expecting bacon and egg every morning, pasties for lunch, chips for dinner. I can't resist. You don't know what it's like, sitting there with a yoghurt and a pile of lettuce watching other people eat. It's awful."

I nodded my agreement. "Yes," I said. "I suppose it's as bad as turning up on a Day Skipper course and people expecting you to be able to sail."

We looked at each other, and both started to laugh at the same time.

"Right then," she said. "Watch me. This is how you do a round turn and two half hitches. Tomorrow we'll make a start on wind direction. As for tonight – I don't suppose one plate of steak and chips will do me that much harm."

I had just managed my first bowline when Sandy returned from the shower block beaming contently.

"At last!" she announced, plonking herself happily on the transom. "Somewhere I can plug my heated curlers in!"

The skipper and I exchanged looks. We were still giggling when the others arrived to see if we were ready for dinner.

Vamos

By Sean Cunningham

A giant walked into my bar last night. What struck me was how he ducked through the doorway. The ceiling at The Hit & Run isn't what I'd call generous. His head poked in first, a shadow, and then the man. All seven foot of man. A stick figure with razor sharp elbows; a thick hairdo perched on this human vessel. The light caught his charcoal skin and he came towards me nose first, wearing a giant sized overcoat and giant sized trousers. The customers looked at him and didn't blink, their revelry on hold.

He stopped behind a couple of regulars at the bar, his midriff level with their heads. They stood with their pints mid-air. He looked at me, then down at them. A moment passed and they parted in the middle. He stepped one step and put this hand on my bar. This skeletal, enormous thing with veins and fingers. The crowd and I stood still and waited for something.

His eyebrows shot upwards when he looked at me. He stood in the silence, put a hand in his fringe and left it there. I looked at it and was going to break the freeze-frame when he said: "Aaaaaaah." A moment of open jaws. He blinked, ruffled the fringe with one hand and slapped the bar with the other. The duo to his sides bounced with the sound. He smiled. "MILK!"

It took a moment for the word to make sense, like the time delay in a live television feed. It was the accent, I think, that and the volume. "Sorry," I said, "Milk?" Some of the more distant customers had begun to lose interest, but the men nearby stayed still.

"Ah," he said, "I would like some milk." A stir of something nearby, close to laughter. I looked to Paul, the manager, who stood frowning, arms crossed, a few feet from me; then back to the giant. I didn't know what to say, so I said "How much milk?" Definite laughter, from more than one of them. The question seemed to stump him so I walked to Paul, who walked to the fridge.

When I came back with the pint of milk he was sitting and the crowd had stirred back to life. I placed it in front of him and tried a genuine grin. "Milk," I said, "There you go my friend."

"Ah, my friend!" The voice burst through the mutters; it sounded Hispanic. A few men stopped and turned to look again. He grabbed the glass and got half of it down. His mouth, outlined in white, smiled an enormous smile.

It was Friday night busy, and the crowd didn't give the spectacle more than a minute of their time. He sat silent, drinking his milk and asking for top ups; and it wasn't until after eleven that he made himself obvious again.

Maria Reilly was sat there with her husband, Neil. A stocky, middle aged man with the face of a jaded Viking. The light made a white globe on his bald head; the face frowned, grimaced, clenched. His conversation had worked itself up, and his voice had an edge to it now. He stared down his pint when he spoke. There wasn't much else to do so I listened.

"They walk about, you do see them," he said.

"You do," she said.

"You can't fuckin' walk anywhere now in town without seeing them."

"They have half of Moore Street now as well. All the shops," she said.

"And I'm not fuckin' being, you know," he looked at her, "but I mean, they're hard enough in small doses."

"Yeah they have all their shops there now."

"I mean, I've no problem with the Polish lads."

"Ah no."

"Or the Russian fellas or anything. But I mean," he gave his pint a look, "you're not Polish, you're not Eastern European. None of that, you're fuckin' black--"

"Yeah," she cut him off nodding, with a quick glance to the giant to their right, "There's nothing wrong with them now, but I mean Jesus Christ." A glass of milk banged down on the bar.

"Ah," the giant moved his head towards Maria, her husband between them, "Jesus!"

I picked up a glass and wiped it with a cloth, inspected it. There was a silence. "Jesus!" I heard again.

"That's right," Neil's voice said "Jesus."

Another pause, then Maria's voice: "Do you like Jesus?"

"Aaaaaah." I glanced up, he was nodding and smiling. He caught my eye a moment. "My friend Jesus Christ. Yes."

"That's very nice," Maria said, "You're a religious man?" The giant stopped nodding.

"Religious?" Maria said again, "Are you religious?" He stared at her with that smile.

"Do you know what that means do you?" Neil said, "Religious? Catholic, protestant. Hindu?"

The giant looked past Neil to his wife.

"You are religious?" he said.

"Me?" She smiled and tucked her chin into her chest. "Well, yes. I would be religious now, I suppose." He gave her a little laugh and she gave it back. They sat smiling at one another and Neil looked at both of them. "What is your name?" Maria asked, tilting her head to one side. The giant took a hit of milk, touched his chest and said: "I am Jorge!"

Paul called my name from the opposite end of the bar. He handed me a stock list and sent me to the cellar.

I was down in the stockrooms, the keg rooms, the fridges, for longer than I should have been. Straining with crates and banging my head in white sterile light; trying to identify lager brands in the scribbles Paul had given me. The giant, Jorge, was there in my head. I imagined him sloped behind me, smiling and looking for the milk. After twenty or so minutes I heard the music. Dull, pulsing bass. Someone had found the jukebox; so underused I'd forgotten it existed.

I thumped the hatch above me twice; heard Paul's "Come up!" I pushed it open and struggled with the crate. It banged heavy on the barroom floor. Crouched over, I gave a sigh and looked at Paul, who was staring out into the lounge. I stood up. The people were looking in one direction, except for Neil, who sat still with his drink.

There in the middle of the room, a big Hispanic man was dancing with a small Irish woman. Their faces were bright with energy, sweat and smiles. The giant danced upright; Maria looking at his chest. Their hair clung to their faces. Some people were laughing, some nodding, but most looked unable to speak.

I was so taken by the display that I hadn't noticed Neil, looking directly at me. I blinked wide-eyed and tried for a friendly expression. "Are you ok there Neil?" I said, "Alright for drinks?"

He stared at me mouth closed. I gave a little nod and tried to act busy, picking up a cloth, wiping the spotless worktop. "Why the fuck do you have the darts on?" Neil said, his voice a dead bass-line. I continued wiping.

"It's the world cup." I said, studying the bar's surface like an archeologist.

"It's fucking darts."

I paused before saying anything; wiped the bar, looked at it, wiped it again.

"You're not mad about the darts then." I said.

"If I was I wouldn't be able to hear the fuckin' thing."

I went to the tap, wet my cloth.

"Would I?" he said, I could feel him eyeing me.

I opened my mouth and looked him in the eye; trying to ooze calm and nice. "It's only a bit of music Neil." I grinned. He clutched his pint with chalk white knuckles. His face told me I shouldn't have grinned.

Podge, an old regular, laughed a low, throaty laugh two seats down. Neil's head pivoted. The man – who wore rags and smelled of the sea – had his back to me, his face to the dancers. His shoulders jostled to a silent chuckle. Neil's head was pointed at him, a face like decaying stone.

"Are you looking at my wife?" he said.

Podge did nothing. Neil brought his pint a seat closer.

"Are you looking at my wife?" he nudged Podge's shoulder with a finger. The man awoke, looked at Neil like a foreign object.

"I'm looking at this thing," he said.

"What thing, where?" Neil said.

"Over –" he made a vague pointing gesture towards the duo, his hand loose like a conductor. He looked at Neil and toyed with a smirk.

Neil looked at the couple. Dancing closer than before, their hands touching thighs and waists. Jorge had her at the small of her back, smiling. Neil's head returned to Podge.

"Thing?" he said, "What thing is that?"

"Ah nothing."

"My wife, is it?"

Podge looked for something neutral to gaze at, found the floor.

"My wife, the thing, is it?" Neil said.

I knew I should do something, but Neil's face kept me silent. Podge paused, head down, then gave the look of a person having solved a riddle and said:

"Would you like a drink?" He waited with a bright expression.

A horn sound sliced through the voices and Jorge grabbed Maria, held her like something precious. The old man watched and Neil watched the old man. He brought his pint eye-level, shot it a hard frown, and swung it at Podge's head. Crack. The sound synced with a bass kick. Glass shattered, Podge dropped. Neil looked down at him, jagged remnants in his hand; the tips pierced red. "You oul pervert," he said, face marked with disgust.

A beat before the bedlam. Then a shriek, and another. A couple of men marched over to where Neil was standing. Eyes wide, posture alert, he aimed for the closer one. The man dodged the swing and pushed Neil towards a stool. Hoarse voices barked, shouts crowded to 'Rock the Boat', trailing along in the background. "What the fuck are you at!" one said. Neil's face was fury crimson, his entire frame trembling.

He looked at the men in front of him, chose one and lunged. His fist glanced the jaw and the man staggered sideways. Neil paused and took a blow to the face. He grabbed the offender close, smacked skulls and the man fell. A gaggle of figures hovered around Neil. Reluctant faces, unsure movements; tired men who disliked action. He took them one by one.

I turned and checked for Paul. He had phone to ear, and shot me a look that expected something. I gave a quick head shake and stared back into the chaos.

A handful of people lay scattered on the floorboards. A semicircle of men panting and looking towards Neil. Grimace on his face, beer stains on his shirt and blood on his hands. Arms and legs spread wide like a sheriff in a Western. His shoulders bounced and a hand fell onto them.

This skeletal, enormous thing with veins and fingers. The shoulder stopped bouncing. The grimace faded, the mouth opened. He stayed frozen in that stance and the room stayed frozen in theirs.

"Aaaaaah." The sound shuddered in the silence. I thought I heard a moan. Neil's skull turned on its axis, sideways and upwards like a robotic doll. A shadow covered it, a fringe dangled loose above.

I noticed Neil's hands; spread wide with fingers so tight

they flickered in the air.

Jorge's head eclipsed the bulb behind it. His face black as a hole in a hole, white teeth gleaming as he smiled a faint smile. His hand squeezed the shoulder, then patted it. Soft and slow. A rumble in his chest, the makings of a laugh.

"Come here," he said. He walked big steps to his seat, bringing Neil with him.

He pulled back the chair and held out a palm. Neil's mouth stayed open, his face a mixture of terror and confusion. He watched Jorge and the Jorge said "Sit."

Neil sat.

We waited and watched. Patient, sweating. Breathing discreetly.

Jorge's arm reached across Neil, who stared at it like you would a weapon. It grabbed the pint glass, half full with milk, and held it at Neil's nose. He took it like something delicate and awaited instruction. A silent second. "Drink." Jorge instructed.

He put it to his mouth and swallowed swallowed swallowed. The thick meat fingers printing lipstick-red blood onto the glass.

Jorge's face beamed, eyes bright. Nodding. The smile so wide it took most of his head. When Neil finished he looked to him.

"I knew one man," Jorge said, eyes on Neil, "he lived so long. One hundred and fifty years old, but he looked one hundred. He drank only milk, ate only bread. Some cheese. Maybe he is still alive."

"You're jokin'," Neil said.

"No." Jorge said. "It's good." Neil nodded with him.

"Fresh." Jorge said.

"Fresh." Neil said. They nodded together and smiled together. Heads bobbing hypnotic. Neil's face seemed loose, almost calm. His eyes wide, looking at this giant like an old friend, teacher, father. Those eyes, sunk into that head, looked like eyes awoken from a coma.

Then, with a small sniff and a shoulder pat, the giant turned and walked. Through bloodied old men, terrified young women; through the path they made for him. He walked to the door of my bar, head floating high. The hint of a siren grew closer as we stared at this giant, Jorge, hunching and disappearing through swinging doors.

The siren screamed and one voice wailed. Maria hurtled herself onto her husband, fists first. Her face buried behind swinging arms, she said: "What the fuck, Neil! What the fuck is wrong with you? What the fuck is wrong with you? What in the name of Jesus –"

He caught both arms and held them midair. His freshly bruised face with those new eyes fixed on her.

"It's ok Maria," he said, voice soft and sure, mouth outlined in white, "it's ok, it's ok." The eyes shone with life, glistened and blinked one blink. "I'm okay now."

A Rose for Remembrance
By Lorraine Mace

I've brought a plant this time, instead of flowers. A remembrance rose, because I don't want you to forget me. Its petals are scarlet, just like the wallpaper you put up in Jenny's first bedroom. I wonder how many women have stood at a graveside and thought as I do. I mean, you're dead and buried, but I can't let you rest. This will be my last visit, though. That's why I thought it would better to plant the rose. I can't believe you've been gone a year. I still see you every time I close my eyes. Smiling, always ready to break into laughter. You were so full of fun.

I expect you're wondering why I'll not be coming back. You'll never guess what I'm going to do. I can hardly credit it myself. I'm going to live in Gibraltar, to be near to our Jenny. This is the last chance I'll have to chat to you – and there's so much I haven't told you yet. I didn't even tell you about our Jenny getting in touch, did I? I didn't really have time before ...

Anyway, she'd phoned and said she wanted to meet. Right out of the blue it was. You've no idea how relieved I was. I wanted her to come home, but she said, no, not yet. Let's meet in the park, Mum. So that's what we did.

Ten years to the day it was, since she'd run away. I almost didn't recognise her. Can you imagine that? Not recognising our only child. She's cut all her hair off, you know, and dyed it red. Red! She does look different. You always loved her long hair and now it's gone. It's a shame you never got the chance to see what a smashing woman she's become. She's like you in many ways, even down to being scared of the dark. She blamed me, you know, said it was my fault she had to leave. You remember how distraught we were when she disappeared? Only fourteen and off she went. Anything could have happened to her. Between you and me, I think a lot did happen. Stuff she hasn't told me about, but maybe she will once I'm over there in Gibraltar with her and her husband, Nick.

There's another thing I never had time to tell you – she was pregnant when we met up again, and she's got a lovely baby girl now. Her husband's great. Really kind and thinks the world of our Jenny. I think you'd have liked him. I bet he'd have liked you. Most people did. You had that nice easy way with you.

Mary from the WI says she's glad I'm going to be living near to family. I think she still worries about me. You remember Mary, don't you? Of course you do. I was on the phone to her when you had your fall. She says she still has nightmares about it. Can still hear you crying out, she says. I'm amazed she heard you as well as she claims. Between you and me, I think she made more of it than she needed to. Still I was glad she was there when it happened. I screamed when I heard you bouncing on the stairs. Threw the receiver up in the air and panicked, just like I always did when anything went wrong.

When I came back to the kitchen I could hear Mary shouting my name. I picked up the receiver and tried to tell her I thought you were dead, but I stumbled over the words. Mary said to put the phone down and she'd call an ambulance. I wanted to tell her not to rush because it was too late, but I just blurted out that you were dead. Mary says it was shock. She could be right. I knew you were gone as soon as I saw the way your neck was all twisted.

When the paramedics arrived one of them said the stairs were an accident waiting to happen. I told him I'd fallen down the day before and he said he could believe that. He asked why the treads were all up and I had to explain about you and your DIY. You were so handy about the place. I told him all about the conservatory and the nice new kitchen you'd put in. He was so kind when he checked me over. Said I was lucky I hadn't suffered more than bruises.

It was the day before your fall that I'd met Jenny. We sat on a bench in the park and talked for hours. She reminded me about how you always called her your princess. When I got back you were on your way out to your youth club meeting. They still miss you, by the way. You were always such an enthusiastic volunteer – always ready to stay late if you needed to. You kissed me goodbye and told me not to wait up. I wanted to tell you where I'd been, but you went rushing out. You grinned and waved. Such a lovely smile. Jenny has it, too. She looks a lot like you, especially now with her short hair. I won't tell her that, though.

She thought I knew – can you believe that? She asked me why I hadn't stopped you. But how could I, when I hadn't known? She said I must have done, but I didn't. You have no idea how many times I've asked myself that question over the last year. How could I miss the signs? But I never guessed. Not for a moment.

I lie awake at night, even now, and wonder. How many others? How many lives did you ruin? Jenny spent years in therapy, she told me. That's why she came back to the UK. To ask why I hadn't stopped you. Why I'd let you do that to her. I was actually sick when she asked me. I puked. Right there in the park. Jenny was great, though. She took care of me. I didn't deserve it. Not after the way I'd let her down.

How could I not have known what you'd done to our baby? She couldn't even remember how old she was when it started. I was always so pleased you wanted to be the one to tuck her up at night. You insisted on doing everything for your princess. I used to tell all my friends how lucky I was to have a husband like you. Can you imagine that?

I thought you'd got involved with the youth club to make up for Jenny running away from home. Well, I suppose I was right, you did.

I'd slipped on the stairs while you were out that evening. That's where the idea came from, but I didn't expect it to work out as well as it did. The next morning, Sunday it was, so I knew you'd have a bit of a lie in, I called Mary as soon as I heard you get up. We talked jam and Jerusalem until I heard you fall. Then I screamed and threw the phone in the air. I took a cushion with me, but I didn't need it. You were already dead. I removed the string before the paramedics arrived.

I was so out of my mind with anger at what you'd done that I didn't need to put on an act. I had to stop you. You do understand that, don't you? I couldn't let you carry on working with those poor children.

Anyway, it's time for me to go. I've done my year of visiting, showed what a dutiful wife I was so that no one would guess. I know you wanted to be cremated and I smiled inside when the wet earth landed on your coffin. I want you to suffer down there in the dark that scared you so. I've planted the rose to hold you in – and for remembrance.

ABOUT THE AUTHORS

Dan Holloway was once, in the same year, officially the most intelligent person in the world and the fourth best discus thrower in Oxford. The quest for "a storyline that makes sense" has, sadly, taken its toll on both of these.

Sean Cunningham is a criminal vandal/sheisty supervillain, currently in hiding from the governments/policemens. He does not have a pet cat, but if he did it would wear a tophat and have a lisp.

Reclusive author Patricia J. DeLois is rumoured to live in Vermont, but in fact she spends most of her time at her home in Maine.

Roland Denning was born in North London a long time ago. He's still there. He's not a Goth.

Jasper Dorgan lives and works in Wiltshire and writes his nights in a garden shed.

Derek Duggan lives in Spain – "He is the best new writing talent I have seen by a country mile," is what award winning author Kazuo Ishiguro had to say about Derek Duggan in a recent dream I had. Kofi Anan had some stuff to say too, but I couldn't hear him over the sound of the banks crumbling. Find him on Facebook.

About the Authors

In his youth, Danny Gillan used to think he was a musician, and played in several bands in and around Glasgow with varying degrees of failure. Now in his late thirties, he accepts that rock godhood is an unlikely eventuality, and has decided to think he is a writer instead. In order to fund this delusion, Danny works in Social Care, supporting adults with learning disabilities. His first novel, Will You Love Me Tomorrow, was published on 1st October, 2008, by Discovered Authors.

Gillian Hamer lives and works around Birmingham as a Company Director in the retail sector, but most weekends heads for the wilds of North Wales where many of her novels are based. After a promising career as a pro-footballer was tragically cut short by a crippling metatarsal injury, her talents turned to her real love of creative writing. A former columnist for Writers' Forum Magazine, she has completed a Writers Bureau course, written three crime/paranormal novels and numerous short stories.

Larry Harkrider lives in Texas, where he spends every spare moment plotting his escape.

JW Hicks - Ancient Celt, scribe and dreamer of the dark.

Amanda Hodgkinson lives and works in south west France as a columnist, travel writer and translator. Her short stories and poetry have appeared in various literary magazines in the UK and USA.

JA Hudspith—Johnny hates bios. He lives in the Shed.

Perry Iles was born in Cambridge (the English one) in 1955. He moved to Scotland in 1991 and now lives near Dumfries with his wife, their daughter and a deranged whippet. He has been writing since last century and is the author of three novels, several short stories and a book about his memories of European travel as a child in the 1960s. He is currently working on his fourth novel, The Other Side of Here. In 2004 his ending to Fay Weldon's One Size Fits All reached the final three in the BBC's End of Story series. Until recently, he worked in the IT industry, but he has now given this up to concentrate on writing full-time. His other interests include travel, modern music, and the sustained abuse of electric guitars.

When Lorraine Mace forgets which country she now lives in, she takes refuge in the Shed.
www.lorrainemace.com

These days, R.K. Nathan lives in Barcelona, having wandered around various parts of the world as a writer, teacher, translator and musician and come full circle, all the way back to the country where his parents met in the Summer of Love.

Lawrence Poole was born in London in 1962 where he still lives, posthumously. His interests include avoiding thought of any kind and his main concern is ensuring his unfinished novel remains unfinished. To this end, he hangs about in the virtual bar at www.bookshed.eu because a) it is the best peer-review site for writers he knows and b) it is the only place that will put up with him.

About the Authors

Nick Poole is a writer, husband, father, Civil Servant, Internet Troll, drunkard, layabout, Socialist, anti-royal, a blinkered chauvinist and like all writers he is both a seeker after truth and a liar.

Jo Reed lives and writes in a leaky house in Somerset, shared with two opinionated Chihuahuas. At certain times of the year she may be found causing mayhem along the Spanish coast with the pointy end of a sailing boat.

Jane Dixon-Smith lives and works in the English Lake District, where she is currently writing a series of novels based on the Warrior Queen, Zenobia, who led the greatest revolt ever staged against Rome.
www.janedixonsmith.co.uk

James Whyle earns his living in Johannesburg, inscribing runes on 64bit Packard Bell electric stone. His play, Rejoice Burning, is available in New South African Plays, Aurora Metro Press.
(www.aurorametro.com/html/ind_books/saplays.html)
He is a founder member of The BookShed.
(www.bookshed.eu)

Cover by Jump'n'Jane
Illustration - Sean Cunningham
Design - Jane Dixon-Smith

www.ingramcontent.com/pod-product-compliance
Ingram Content Group UK Ltd.
Pitfield, Milton Keynes, MK11 3LW, UK
UKHW041257180426
11947UKWH00008B/542